HOLD MY HEART

Romancing The Heirs Book Five

K.S. ELLIS

Copyright © 2024 K.S. Ellis
All rights reserved

The characters and events portrayed in this book are fictitious. Any similarity to real persons, living or dead, is coincidental and not intended by the author.

No part of this book may be reproduced, or stored in a retrieval system, or transmitted in any form or by any means, electronic, mechanical, photocopying, recording, or otherwise, without express written permission of the publisher.

ISBN: 9798390639283
Imprint: Independently published
Editor: Mimsy's Words Proofreading & Editing Services

Sometimes the best people in our lives come into them as adversaries. Don't write them off just yet.

ACKNOWLEDGMENTS

And it's done. The Romancing the Heirs series, which started as a dream about a PA and a billionaire hooking up on vacation in England spawned a whole series. I am toying with a small novella of Uncle Bill's POV, but I'm not sure I'm ready to leap out of my comfort zone of writing MMCs and FMCs that much older than me. I don't know if I can get into their heads the same way, and I'm not going to write something if I'm not 100% sure I can do them justice. I have the outline though, so never say never.

Cameron, your support has been life-changing. From encouraging me to finish my first book, to being my first beta reader and proof-reader, to my biggest champion. Thank you. I would still be an unpublished dreamer if it wasn't for you.

To everyone who read this book, suggested tweaks and edits and made it so much better – thank you! We did it! Here's to the next series.

To all my readers, we're saying goodbye to the Westerhavens (for now), but never say never, and as I like to thread all my different series together in the same universe, we may see them again soon! I hope you have loved this series as much as I have. I will miss them, but onto the next!

More by K.S. Ellis

SAN REMO SINNERS COLLECTION:
WILD HAWKS MC:

Sweet Sin

Sweet Torture

Sweet Pain

Sweet Redemption

Wild Hawks MC Boxset

HAWKS INK:

Mark Me

Make Me

Miss Me

Hawks Ink Boxset

BROTHERS OF THE WILD HAWKS:

Buster

Palmer

Merch

Viper

Brothers of the Wild Hawks Boxset

SEATTLE SIZZLES COLLECTION:

Falling For You

Just Like That

Lie With Me

BAD BOYS OF BOSTON

THE IRISH:

Born to be Bad

Bad Blood

Bad to the Bone

Bad Luck

Bad at Heart

Bad at Last

The Irish Boxset

ROMANCING THE HEIRS:

Hold Me Tight

Never Let Me Go

Love Me Well

Stay With Me

Hold My Heart

Romancing the Heirs Boxset

LA LOVERS COLLECTION:

The Marine & Me

FREE GIVEAWAY:

Hacking Agent Yummy

CONTENTS

	PROLOGUE	Pg 1
1	CHAPTER ONE	Pg 8
2	CHAPTER TWO	Pg 16
3	CHAPTER THREE	Pg 25
4	CHAPTER FOUR	Pg 34
5	CHAPTER FIVE	Pg 45
6	CHAPTER SIX	Pg 57
7	CHAPTER SEVEN	Pg 66
8	CHAPTER EIGHT	Pg 77
9	CHAPTER NINE	Pg 84
10	CHAPTER TEN	Pg 92
11	CHAPTER ELEVEN	Pg 106
12	CHAPTER TWELVE	Pg 119
13	CHAPTER THIRTEEN	Pg 128
14	CHAPTER FOURTEEN	Pg 140

15	CHAPTER FIFTEEN	Pg 157
16	CHAPTER SIXTEEN	Pg 171
17	CHAPTER SEVENTEEN	Pg 177
18	CHAPTER EIGHTEEN	Pg 187
19	CHAPTER NINETEEN	Pg 195
20	CHAPTER TWENTY	Pg 201
21	CHAPTER TWENTY-ONE	Pg 209
22	CHAPTER TWENTY-TWO	Pg 218
23	CHAPTER TWENTY-THREE	Pg 228
24	CHAPTER TWENTY-FOUR	Pg 234
25	CHAPTER TWENTY-FIVE	Pg 241
26	CHAPTER TWENTY-SIX	Pg 249
27	CHAPTER TWENTY-SEVEN	Pg 264
28	CHAPTER TWENTY-EIGHT	Pg 274
29	CHAPTER TWENTY-NINE	Pg 282
30	CHAPTER THIRTY	Pg 288
	EPILOGUE	Pg 295

I hate him. Except for all the places where I love him half to death.

Charlotte Stein

Prologue

Layla

Smoothing my hands on my skirt for about the millionth time, I take a deep breath, counting to ten, hoping to calm my rapidly pounding heart. I was so proud of myself when I was promoted to junior manager at Haven Freight last year. I think I've done a good job. I've had nothing but praise from the managers above me, and I've had no complaints from staff under me or customers I work with.

But I'm still nervous as all hell. It started two weeks ago. I got an email in my work inbox. It looked innocuous enough – from Haven Enterprises, so... part of the Haven Group – I thought it was a memo or something.

It was *not* a memo. It was an invitation for an all-expenses paid trip to Chicago to attend an HR event at Haven Enterprises' offices. And I mean ALL expenses paid. I flew business class. *Business class*. I've never even been that far up the front of a plane before. Hell, I'd barely left San Diego for a hot minute.

The email said it was an HR networking event, but I haven't met another soul apart from Cathy Milleneau. She said she's a "PA," yet everyone defers to her, so I don't know whose PA she is… but I bet they're important. She left me here with a fancy coffee and a smile, promising to be right back. That was half an hour ago. My coffee is finished, my palms are sweaty, and everyone looks sideways at me as they walk past.

Before I can get any further up in my head, the door beside me opens, and I jump a mile. Cathy's warm, low laugh washes over me. "Hey there, jumpy. We're ready for you."

Ready for me? Crap. Was I supposed to be in there ages ago? She told me to wait. Standing, I pray my knees won't give out. They wobble, but I stay upright. Thank God. Cathy takes my coffee cup, leading me through a large, airy room with two desks. She leaves the empty cup on the slightly messier one, waving to the young woman sitting at the other. The other woman's eyes flicker over me with interest as we continue to another room.

I blink, frozen on the spot, as Cathy moves aside to reveal the man sitting at the desk in the large, sunlit room. Crap. *Crap.* It's Bill Westerhaven. The billionaire. The head of the entire Haven Group. Do you know who else is in the room? No one. Not a single soul.

The door gently swings shut behind me, and it's me, Cathy, and Bill freaking Westerhaven. He stands, looking sharp as a silver fox in his gray suit, his dark, intelligent eyes cursorily assessing me. With a small smile, he gestures, open palm up, at the two comfortable-looking chairs in front of his huge, highly polished, hardwood desk.

"Ms. Hall, please, take a seat."

Cathy has already seated herself off to the side, an iPad out, her legs crossed, watching me expectantly. When my eyes dart to her, she smiles encouragingly and nods to the seat. Forcing my feet to unstick from the ground, I hurry over, almost stumbling as I sink into the chair, gripping my hands tightly in my lap. Mr. Westerhaven smiles again – more of a smirk this time – and slowly resumes his seat.

He rests his elbows on the arms of his leather chair, steepling his fingertips in front of his mouth as he studies me silently. I refuse to move my hands from my lap. The urge to smooth them on my skirt again is riding me hard, but I don't want them to know I have sweaty palms. How embarrassing.

Finally, Mr. Westerhaven speaks again. "Ms. Hall. I've heard nothing but good things about you from Haven Freight."

Flames dance across my cheeks. I'm as pale as a vampire – the San Diego sun has never done much for me, despite living there my whole life – so I'm sure I'm going to be lobster red. Double embarrassment.

"Th-thank you. I'm enjoying the work."

We lapse into silence as Mr. Westerhaven nods thoughtfully. "I'm glad to hear that. Have you ever thought of a career change?"

A… what? My eyes widen, my cheeks an inferno now. "I-I'm sorry?"

Am I being fired? Was I flown all the way to Chicago and put up in a five-star hotel to be fired personally by Bill Westerhaven? How badly do you have to screw up for that to happen? How the hell did I manage this?

"I-I…" I have no idea what to say. What the hell *am* I supposed to say to that?

Mr. Westerhaven grimaces as though realizing how his words actually sounded. "What I meant was, have you ever given any thought to moving to another business in the Haven Group?"

My cheeks cool the tiniest amount. Okay, so not totally fired. But who did I piss off to be run out of San Diego? I offer a noncommittal smile as I try to run through every imaginable scenario in my head to work out who I unintentionally offended.

"Uh, I can't say I've ever given it much thought. I grew up in San Diego. I enjoy my job at Haven Freight. Leaving has never occurred to me."

Mr. Westerhaven nods again, still studying me carefully. "We wouldn't want to uproot your life too much. We thought perhaps you might be well suited to a role that has opened up in LA at Haven Pharmaceuticals."

HOLD MY HEART

Okay. So I'm not being banished to New York. That's nice to know. "LA is nice. I've been a few times on vacations."

Mr. Westerhaven's smile is back, encouraged by my lack of a flat-out refusal. Like I would flat-out refuse. I'm being moved for a reason. I've clearly clashed with *someone* important. Saying no would probably see me straight-up fired.

"As I said, I've heard nothing but glowing reviews about your work and how you fit with a team. I think this role would be perfect for you."

I'm blushing again. But that's because a billionaire businessman said I did well at work. How silly is that?

Mr. Westerhaven gestures to Cathy's iPad. "We'll have to assess some aspects of your approach to things. Just to ensure you are a good fit. Cathy is going to email you some scenarios. Think of them as problem-solving exercises. I think four days would be sufficient. If you could prepare reports to be presented on each scenario, we will meet back here in four days to hear them."

Oh my god. I think this is a proper job interview. A four-day long one. This is weird. But hell yeah, I'm going to seize this opportunity with both hands. I smile as he stands, and shove to my feet as well, eagerly reaching for his hand when he extends it across the expanse of the desk. He shakes it firmly, turning to gesture to the door. "I look forward to seeing what you come up with, Ms. Hall. I have a good feeling about you."

Okay. That's... nice. A little strange, but still nice. I throw him a smile. "Thank you so much for this opportunity, Mr. Westerhaven."

With a nod, he flicks his hand dismissively. I hurry to the door, following Cathy out.

"I'll walk you out of the building," she announces cheerfully, flashing her office companion a smile as she guides me through the room and out into the corridor.

I follow her along, fidgeting with my skirt once again. Cathy's eyes drop to it, and she smiles. "You'll do great. Just think of it like an exercise back in San Diego. Enjoy the sights and take your laptop. Get inspiration. I know you're going to do amazing."

Nodding, I wave her off, clutching my purse to my chest as I slide into the town car Cathy pointed to. My heart is thudding as we glide through the city traffic to my opulent hotel.

Hurrying across the marble-floored lobby and up to my incredible room, I ignore the sumptuous surroundings, digging my laptop out and dropping onto the small, golden fabric couch as I open my work email, my hands shaking. I click on the email from Catherine Milleneau, my eyes darting over the questions. My breath blows out, and my shoulders sag in relief. They're management problems. Thank goodness, I know nothing about pharmaceuticals.

They're more top-level, whole company management issues, but that's okay. Maybe they want to make sure I can work with a large team in mind rather than the small one of three people I manage. I can do this. I have four days.

Kicking off my shoes, I ring down to order some room service – hold the wine; I need to be sharp – and set my laptop up at the polished wooden desk overlooking the incredible cityscape view. Stretching my neck, I open a new text document, reading through the question carefully. I'm going to nail this. If I'm moving to LA, I'm doing it not because I'm being exiled, but because I'm the right damn person for the job.

Chapter One

Layla

Smoothing my hand over the table runner, I take a deep breath, looking around in satisfaction. My home has been transformed by the best catering company I have ever interacted with. This place looks amazing. I catch my snort. Of course, this place looks amazing. I lived in a studio apartment back in San Diego. I can't believe this is my home now in LA. Stepping into the kitchen, I offer Marielle, the head caterer, a smile. My eyes linger on the trashcan tucked in the corner of the room, waiting to be filled with used napkins as canapes are passed around and consumed tonight.

It reminds me of another trashcan back in San Diego. The head of HR at Haven Enterprises had flown all the way to San Diego to offer me a job here at Haven Pharmaceuticals. I was intrigued until I read the offer letter she handed over. Then I hurled into the trashcan. I was mortified. She was, thankfully, amused. She merely handed me a bottle of water and a box of tissues and ran me through the logistics of my new role. It wasn't a junior management role. It wasn't even a senior management role. I thought I was being pranked.

Hold My Heart

I signed on the dotted line faster than I've ever done anything in my life. I am now officially the COO – Chief Operating Officer – of Haven Pharmaceuticals. I answer to no one but the Haven Pharmaceuticals Board (officially) and Bill Westerhaven (unofficially).

Of course, in addition to the shock, I was also suffering from severe impostor syndrome. I was a junior manager! How could they think I was suitable for the position of COO? I almost tore my signature back off the page until they handed me the lovely letter from Mr. Westerhaven. I still have it framed in a drawer in my dressing table upstairs. He wrote to me, personally urging me to take the position. He assured me that my job offer was based solely on the solutions I presented to their problem-solving issues.

Apparently, they are very real issues Haven Pharmaceuticals is facing. In the month between my accepting the job offer and starting work here in LA, they have been executing my solutions at the company and wanted me present to oversee the implementation.

Of course, the job was only the beginning. After I signed that contract, everything felt like it was rushing along at warp speed. I was paid a "generous signing bonus" – read four times my annual salary – and even a moving bonus to help relocate to LA. Back in San Diego, I lived in a rented, *furnished* studio apartment. Everything I owned fit into four suitcases. I took my ridiculous bonuses, hopped on a plane, and bought this amazing condo.

I sigh happily as I move back through the cream and pine space. Twinkling lights are wound around the banister, making the area seem magical. I've been at Haven Pharmaceuticals for two weeks now. I have my very own PA, Karly Wright, and *the biggest office I have ever set foot in.* Not only that, but the staff and board seem enthusiastic about my new policies. Pinch me because I *must* be dreaming.

The only person on the management team I haven't met is Ryan Pierce Westerhaven. He is one of Bill Westerhaven's famous five nephews and heirs. He hasn't been in LA while I have. One of his Westerhaven cousins was getting married, making it necessary for him to be in Chicago for three weeks to party or whatever.

I've never been to a three-week party. It sounds exhausting. Though, I have been embarking on a week of my own parties – which is grueling, especially as I'm hosting.

Karly lets herself into the condo with a huge grin. "They're arriving. Action stations!"

Fixing my smile, I collect a glass of champagne off the tray of a waiter who has magically appeared from my new, shiny kitchen. I wanted to be an approachable COO, so I've been hosting a different Haven Pharmaceuticals team each night, trying to get to know everyone at the management level.

The door opens, and the first guests step inside. Widening my smile, I hold out my hand. "Welcome! Come in and make yourself at home. I'm Layla. I can't wait to hear all about your roles and vision for Haven Pharmaceuticals."

Their smiles are wide as they accept champagne from my waiter, moving inside as I turn to greet the next arrivals. Did you know that if you throw parties for your staff, the business pays for all your champagne and catering? Even for cleaning up? I had no idea. I thought – and the board agreed – that it's a small price to pay to hear everyone's opinions and suggestions. These people are a goldmine of ideas waiting to be heard. I want to amplify them as loudly as I can.

Ryan

Stifling a yawn, I nod to the driver as I climb out of the town car. He collects my suitcases, leaving them near the door before sliding into the car and driving off. It's mid-afternoon on a gloriously sunny LA day, but I'm not due back in the office until tomorrow. Getting together with the boys is always a hell of a good time. It doesn't happen nearly as much as it should. As it is, they're all married now. Timmy's a father, and David's wife is about to pop with twins. Still, those boys were still up for a few nights out.

I could sleep for a week, but in reality, I'll be up early tomorrow to work out and hit the office with my feet moving. After three weeks away, my inbox is going to be looking *rough*. I told my PA, Andy, to only contact me if it was an emergency. Nothing appears to have come up, so that's good news.

There's a staircase from the garage level up, but I hit the elevator. I'm not humping two suitcases up those stairs. I stop at the first level, leaving my bags inside the door to my bedroom. I'll go through them and leave whatever needs to be washed for my cleaning staff when they come through in two days.

I don't bother with the elevator now I have unburdened myself of my suitcases, taking the stairs two at a time. I bypass the second level – I'm not about to raid the fridge. I'll order something in later – and jog up to the top level, stepping out onto the artificial grass near my infinity pool. The sun is beating down, but I'm not here to swim. I pour myself a glass of ice-cold water at the large outdoor wet bar and drop onto the spacious couch, my eyes finding the view.

When I first saw my Hollywood Hills home, I made an offer immediately. Built into the side of the steep slope, the three levels rise out of the ground in sleek, metal lines. All the rooms soak in the views, with walls entirely of glass. When I choose to, I can set the glass to blackout, but I mainly like to keep them clear when I'm home. What's the point of having a multi-million-dollar view if you're not going to look at it every chance you get?

Fishing my phone out of my pocket, I open my emails, scrolling through them, working out what order I want to tackle them in. One from Andy catches my eye. It was sent a week ago. **Not urgent, but important.**

I click on it with a frown, my eyes darting over the contents. In no time at all, I surge off the couch.

"What the *fuck*?" I spit, throwing my glass into the wet bar's sink. I barely notice the shattering glass, striding to the stairs and jogging down them all the way to the garage. My Range Rover Evoque is the closest, so I grab the keys, sling myself inside, and slam my phone into the cradle as I reverse out of the building, my tires squealing when I stomp on the gas.

Uncle Bill answers on the fourth ring. "Ryan?"

"Who the *fuck* is Layla Hall?" I snap, weaving through the early afternoon traffic, leaving a trail of honking horns and irate drivers in my wake.

"She's Haven Pharmaceuticals' new COO," Uncle Bill replies mildly like we're discussing where to have a long summer lunch.

"Why is Andy emailing me that Layla Hall is implementing *changes* while I'm gone?" I snarl, cutting off a dark SUV as I hurtle around a corner.

"Because the board and I authorized the changes, and as Layla Hall is the mastermind and the new COO, she's overseeing them."

"*I'm* on the board. I didn't authorize shit!"

"You are one member and one vote. You were not required to be present."

My teeth grind together as I breathe heavily through my nose. This is Uncle Bill pulling rank. I don't know what the fuck I did to deserve this shit, but apparently, I'm being taught a lesson. I don't fucking like it.

"When did we even get a COO?" I'm sullen, but I don't care.

"The offer was made to Ms. Hall a month ago. She happily accepted and started in her role two weeks ago."

Right when I was in Chicago. This was planned. God, Uncle Bill is a sneaky prick.

"What changes?"

My knuckles turn white as Uncle Bill details a list before ending the call. A very specific list. A list of four items that I was planning to look into this week now that I'm back from Beau's wedding. That list, in that order, was saved in my emails. Someone has gone in and retrieved it to hand to this Layla Hall. That's unacceptable.

The Evoque's tires squeal again as I pull up at the security gate at Haven Pharmaceuticals.

"Mr. Pierce Westerhaven. Welcome back. How was Chicago?"

I glance at the security guard, a muscle working in my jaw. "It was great. It's even better to be back."

The man smiles vaguely, waving me through the gate. I resist the urge to slam my foot on the gas, driving at a slower, more measured pace to my parking spot. There is an empty spot two down. The engraved plaque reads **Layla Hall, COO.**

Good. The woman isn't even here. I'll have all her policies undone before she returns from her long lunch or wherever she's fucked off to.

Chapter Two

Ryan

Andy looks up in surprise as I storm into the office. "I thought you weren't back until tomorrow, Mr. Pierce Westerhaven?"

Shooting him a lethal glare, I stomp into my office, waiting until he hurries in after me, the glass door swinging shut.

"Not urgent? How the *fuck* is some COO coming in and changing *everything* not fucking urgent? You should have called me about that shit."

Andy pales, shifting his feet. "Mr. Westerhaven said it wasn't urgent enough for you to be disturbed."

My teeth click with how fast they slam together. Fucking Uncle Bill. What the hell is he playing at? I might like to party, but I'm fucking *amazing* at my job, and he knows it. I run this place tighter than a Navy ship.

When Andy doesn't speak, I fill the silence for him. "Well? Where did she fuck off to?"

Andy starts to speak, catching himself, frowning, and resetting. "Nowhere. She's in her office."

A muscle jumps in my jaw. "Her car space is empty."

Andy's lips twitch. "She takes the bus."

HOLD MY HEART

She fucking *what*? What the hell is the COO of Haven Pharmaceuticals doing taking the fucking *bus* to work? Andy gestures toward the door. "She's set up in the empty office suite near the boardroom. I can access her calendar. I don't believe she has any meetings scheduled at the moment. I can check."

"That's not necessary."

Andy stares after me, mouthing like a fish as I storm out of the room. My feet turn right, heading for the boardroom. Sure enough, the glass embossed door of the office suite past it at the end of the hall now reads **Layla Hall, Chief Operating Officer**.

Gritting my teeth, I shove the door open and step inside. The suite mirrors my own, the two offices bookending the entire floor. The antechamber desk is occupied by a bespectacled, mousy little woman who leaps to her feet.

"Mr. Pierce Westerhaven! We heard you weren't back until tomorrow. How was Chicago?"

I frown at her. I don't recognize her. Has she always worked here? "Are you new?"

Her cheeks flame red, her eyelashes fluttering rapidly. That has to be a nervous gesture.

"I-I'm Karly Wright. I-I've been in the secretary pool for three years."

Oh. Whatever. "Where is Layla Hall?"

Karly blinks, her hand trembling as she gestures toward the internal door. "I'll j-just see if she's f-free."

Oh, no. Offering a half-smile, I don't bother to wait for her to alert Ms. Hall to my presence, striding to the internal glass door and stepping through, closing it behind me. This is between us, not for PAs to gossip about.

The layout here is identical to mine, the furniture fairly generic, with some personal touches here and there, like she's still making the space her own. There's no need for that. I'll have her out of here with her tail between her legs before she has a chance to get too comfortable. My gaze immediately lands on the woman seated behind the desk. She looks up as I stride in, her eyes widening. The look of surprise disappears quickly, schooled into a neutral expression as she slowly rises.

My eyes dip to take in her outfit. The only thought that comes to mind is "prissy." She would be a few years younger than me. Mid-twenties, with masses of thick dark brown hair, pale skin, and a blouse and pinafore combo that wouldn't be out of place on a 1950s Catholic schoolgirl. *This* is the COO Uncle Bill chose to torment me with? Is this a fucking joke? The woman looks like a parody of a schoolteacher. Not to mention she's short. Pixie like. I am going to feel ridiculous arguing about company policies with someone who looks like breathing on her wrong would snap her in half.

Hold My Heart

I'm still going to argue with her about them. This is my company, and she has no right to come in here and *change* things without my authority.

"Mr. Pierce Westerhaven?" she guesses drily. Fuck, even her voice is pixie-like. Not squeaky, but melodic, like she's almost singing at me.

"Ryan," I snap back at her. There's no way I'm going head-to-head with someone who takes the time to call me *Mr. Pierce Westerhaven* every few sentences. Nothing ruins the flow of a good argument like deference. She blinks in surprise, nodding, but I wave my hand dismissively. That's not what I'm here to talk about. Let's get to the point, shall we?

"How did you get the list of management issues out of my emails?"

Her eyes widen again, a tiny line appearing between them. "I was hired to implement solutions to those problems."

"Oh, so when they're fixed, you're going to fuck off?"

Her head snaps back like I've slapped her. Okay, maybe that was a bit harsh, but she's the one coming in here touching *my* issues at *my* company. Her voice is less melodic and steelier when she speaks, her eyebrows floating up her forehead.

"As far as I am aware, my position is permanent and not based on a set workload. I'm afraid you'll be stuck with me for a while."

Oh, that won't be happening. If I can't fire her, I'll drive her out. Either way, she's not staying long-term. A smirk tugs at my lips as I cross my arms over my chest, and she mirrors the action. "I don't need a COO to come in here, meddling with how I run this company and implementing solutions that haven't been vetted. What is your experience in the pharmaceutical industry?"

"I-I'm a manager. That's my experience. The industry doesn't matter. I wasn't hired to look after the pharmaceutical side of things."

Gotcha. "So, you have zero experience in the industry, and now you're here implementing issues to pharmaceutical-specific industry-wide issues."

"I have been hired because I actually had solutions for those issues. Solutions the board has reviewed and approved. Do *they* have pharmaceutical experience?"

"Some of them. That's why they were hired. More to the point, *I* have pharmaceutical experience. A whole fucking degree in it. This is my industry and my company, and you're intruding, offering unwanted and unnecessary solutions."

Her mouth drops open, her hands mimicking its open-and-shut movement. My smirk widens. There's nothing she can say to that logic, and she knows it. I have her cornered. She might as well quit now.

Hold My Heart

Layla

Okay. What? When he walked in, it was obvious who he was and that he wasn't entirely happy that I had been hired to implement my solutions while he was absent. I'm not sure why he didn't know about me. I thought that would all have been discussed. But family dynamics aside, I was hired by the board. My solutions were reviewed and approved by the board. He has no right to storm in here spewing vitriol. I don't care how relaxed and handsome he looks in his jeans and a white T-shirt that stretches over his sculpted chest.

Ugh. Why am I even noticing that? He's come in here, hostile as all hell, and he *cannot* speak to me like that. He just can't. He better not have talked to Karly like that. I'll tear him a new asshole if he did. It's unacceptable. What kind of horrible person speaks with such hate toward someone they've never met before? I was here willing to work with him. If he had just *asked*, I would explain that Bill Westerhaven hired me *specifically* for those four issues.

But you know what? He's an ass, and there's no reasoning with tiny-dicked pricks like him. Fuck that strategy. He wants a fight? He's going to get one. And I'm going to fight tooth and nail. Bring it. Step One – shutting him up. Fixing him with an icy glare, I let his rude words flow over me. I need to let him know that I'm rising to this challenge, and if he thinks I'm just going to run away and cry, he is very much mistaken. You picked the wrong woman to fight with.

"I'm here because I've earned this position, thank you very much. Not because of nepotism."

I could almost giggle at the abrupt change in his demeanor. His mouth stops making sounds but stays open for a moment before snapping shut with an audible noise. Ouch. His teeth must be rattling after that. Words have more effect if you don't crowd them, so I don't bother to seize the moment to rant back at him. We're still standing with our arms crossed over our chests, glaring at each other. My chest is heaving, and my heart is racing faster than a hummingbird's wings.

Ryan is still staring at me, a muscle jumping in his jaw, his bright blue eyes like Bunsen burner flames burning my face. Shit. Please don't blush – that would totally take the sting out of my words.

My face stays blessedly pale, my outward appearance not giving away my inner turmoil. Finally, Ryan drops his arms, turns on his heel, and storms out without a word. The second the door closes behind him, I drop until I'm squatting on the ground, my arms wrapped around me, breathing deeply to calm my racing heart.

Oh, the adrenaline rush of staring him down feels good. But, simultaneously, slight anxiety is rising in my mind. What if he complains to his uncle, and I find myself out on my ass? I can't get fired. I love my job. Karly bursts into the room, and my head snaps up at the sound of her crashing footsteps. Her eyes are wide, her mouth open.

"Are you okay?" she squeaks. I blink up at her. Oh, right. The floor/ball thing.

Slowly, I stand, straightening, and flashing her a confident smile. Honestly, I am on top of the world right now. I think I won that encounter.

"I'm fine. I put him in his place."

Karly blinks at me for a moment, her lips twitching, giggles bursting from them. She presses her fingers against her mouth, but it doesn't stop the infectious sounds from spilling out. My lips tug upward into a grin, and before I know it, I'm laughing too.

"Do you think I'm going to be fired?" I manage to get out through giggles. Karly shakes her head.

"I don't think he can do that without the board's approval. They like you. So does Mr. Westerhaven."

"He might like me a bit less when he hears what I said to his nephew."

Karly shrugs, swallowing more giggles. "Would Mr. Pierce Westerhaven go running to his uncle telling tales?"

The idea brings me up short. While he came across as entitled and angry, I didn't get the vibe off Ryan that he goes running to his uncle to fix his problems. I hope he doesn't. This is between us. Everyone else can butt out.

Chapter Three

Ryan

Andy watches me with expectant, raised eyebrows as I storm back to my suite. Shooting him a glare that leaves no room for interpretation – I don't want to be interrupted – I stride into my office, snapping the door shut. As much as you can snap a glass door that doesn't have a locking mechanism shut. Sinking into the sleek gray sofa, I stare out the window, my mind jumbled with various annoyed, furious, and irritated thoughts. I catch one, musing on it, anger surging through me.

I can't believe she implied I'm just some party playboy. I can't believe she straight up said she thinks I'm no good at my job and only got it because I'm a Westerhaven. I'll show her. Shoving off the couch, I stalk to my desk, drop into the chair, and fire up the computer. I have a backlog of emails to get through. I need to get started, so I can clear them out and throw everything into this war with Layla Hall.

My eyes land on an email forwarded from Uncle Bill. It's a generic one, some memo about a symposium. Now I'm annoyed at *two* people. Uncle Bill planned this. My fingers flex on the keyboard. Fuck. Does *Uncle Bill* think I'm nothing but a playboy partier? Did he only give me this job because

I'm a Westerhaven – not because he thought I would be good at it?

Groaning, I grind my eyes with the heels of my palm before they dart to the clock. It's 6 PM in New York right now. I click on the video chat, hitting David's name. He answers after five rings. I frown at the background. That isn't his office at Haven Property. He left Chicago the day before I did, so he should be back at work already.

"Hey, man. What's up?"

"You're not at work."

David glances around at his condo, his lips twitching. "Ani's pregnant with twins."

Yeah, I know. He was bragging to everyone at Max's wedding, and she was already huge at Beau's.

"She has a couple of months to go. Why does that mean you aren't at work?"

David rolls his eyes, smirking at me. "Twins are usually born a little early, and she's 32 weeks. We had to get a letter from her OBGYN to fly to Chicago for the wedding."

"So… you're just working at home until she pops?"

"Uh, yeah. You're damn right I am. I'm not getting stuck in rush hour traffic and missing out on my kids being born." David frowns, leaning closer to the camera. "Why are you at work? I thought you weren't going back until tomorrow?"

I shrug, slumping back in my chair. "Had some issues I had to sort out."

"Oh. Did you get them sorted?"

My face darkens as I remember Layla's last words, and a scowl crosses my face. David's eyebrows shoot up at the sight.

"That looks like a no face. What's going on?"

"Do you think Uncle Bill gave me this job because I'm his nephew?"

"Yes."

My stomach twists, bile rising in my throat at how easily and quickly David answers. He gestures around him.

"He literally started five businesses because he has five nephews. These jobs are for us."

Oh. That's not what I meant. I sigh, pinching the bridge of my nose. "No. I mean… do you think he sees me as nothing but a playboy who likes to party, and I just got given Haven Pharmaceuticals because that was the last business? Because I'm the youngest, and he'd allocated the rest to you lot already?"

David's eyebrows shoot up so fast and high they almost leave his face entirely as his mouth twists into a scowl.

"What the fuck is this? Imposter syndrome? Uncle Bill had this crap picked out since we were in middle school. You were all over that STEM shit. That's why you got the pharmaceutical company. He had it all picked out before Timmy hit high school. You got your company because you were the best one of us for it."

I open my mouth to put forward another argument, but David is on a roll now, cutting me off before I can even get a word out. "There's no Westerhaven wing of a library at Duke. Uncle Bill didn't lay down any cash to get you into that school. You did it on your merit. He didn't pay anyone off to get you your 4.0 GPA or summa cum laude graduation honors. What's brought this on?"

I feel a little better after David's pep talk, and I feel stupid for letting Layla's words get to me. What does she know? She has no idea how hard I worked to get here. I had to fight *against* the Westerhaven name as much as I reaped benefits from it. Having a name like Westerhaven means you can't coast on it. Ever. Because people like Layla will automatically assume everything is handed to you because of your name and you did nothing to earn it yourself.

David's right. I worked my *ass* off to be where I am today. Uncle Bill isn't a sentimental fool. He wouldn't have handed it over to me if I wasn't up to this job. Straightening my shoulders, I smirk at David.

"Thanks, man. It was just a moment of self-doubt."

David grins. "We all have them."

HOLD MY HEART

"You thought you weren't the best choice for Haven Property once upon a time?"

"Uh. No. I'm fucking *amazing* at this shit. Uncle Bill knew what he was doing placing me here. My moment was with Ani."

"With Ani? You had self-doubt with *Ani*?"

David's face darkens, a growl rumbling out of him. "Choose your next words carefully. That's my fucking wife."

Shit. I backpedal quickly. "I just meant… she's crazy about you. What's to doubt?"

David seems appeased – that was close – and shrugs. "I let her go. I let her go home to Chicago without telling her how I felt. Without asking her to pick me. Because I thought I wasn't good enough for her. That I didn't deserve her."

"That's bullshit. You two are perfect together."

A goofy grin tugs at David's mouth. "Yeah, we are."

"Ugh, I'm signing off now."

"Good. I'm going to go find my wife and -"

"I don't need to know!" I yell, ending the call so his grinning face disappears from the screen. Blowing out a breath, I slump back in my chair, scrubbing my face and staring at the ceiling. David is right. I've fucking got this. Layla Hall doesn't stand a chance.

Layla

Hooking my purse over my wrist, I shove my condo door open, sighing as I kick the door shut. Blessed silence reigns through the space. My bag makes a jarring thud as it hits the polished pine flooring, but I leave it where it lies. I need wine. So much wine.

Stooping only to snatch up my cell phone, I stomp into the kitchen, snagging the half-empty bottle of red wine from the fridge and a large glass from the upper cabinets. My phone buzzes from where it lies on the granite countertop. I glance over, twisting my lips into a grimace as I turn back to my glass, not stopping until it is full to the brim.

I tuck my phone into my bra, carefully collecting my wineglass with both hands, making my way out to the small porch overlooking my postage-stamp backyard. The space is only large enough for a small table and two chairs. It's all I need, one to sit on and one to prop my feet on. Setting the glass down, I sink into the left seat, kicking off my heels and resting my feet on the second chair. I dump the cell on the table, turning eagerly to my glass, and taking a sip as it sits on the surface.

There. That's low enough not to slosh over the edges when I pick it up. Sitting back, I sigh, staring at the low fence and patchy grass. I need a gardener. Nothing fancy, just someone to prune the hedges, keep the smattering of shrubs and flowers alive, and make sure the grass doesn't turn into a mud pit. I have only ever lived in apartments. I don't know how to keep living things alive. I don't even trust myself to get a goldfish.

My eyes drift to my phone again, lying innocently on the table. Groaning, I snatch it up, opening Karly's messages.

KARLY: Are you OK?

KARLY: He's a dick. Everyone knows that.

KARLY: Call me if you need to talk.

Sighing, I tap back a message, letting the phone drop back onto the table.

LAYLA: I'm fine. I'm not worried about rich playboys who get their jobs from their uncles.

Plucking my wineglass back up, I take a sip, my gaze lingering on the fence again. So, that was Ryan Pierce Westerhaven. He's exactly the spoiled dick I thought he was going to be. No surprises there. I'm also not surprised that he doesn't like me coming in and making changes. He has probably had unchecked power at Haven Pharmaceuticals for far too long. That's probably why they've been having these management issues. Or, at the very least, why the problems haven't been dealt with until now.

Maybe he's just jealous because my ideas are going to work, and they're being implemented, and he wasn't able to swoop in and take credit. I've heard these nepotism types like doing that. It's the only way they look like they're contributing – stealing everyone else's ideas and passing them off as their own.

Well, he can suck it up. Mr. Westerhaven asked me about these issues directly. He had time to consider them and hired me to implement them. Ryan was never going to be able to take credit. Plus, I have the remit of the board. I was *grilled* over these issues to make sure they were watertight. I passed with flying colors. I wonder how often Ryan Pierce Westerhaven can say that. Probably not a lot. If he's not paying for it, he probably barely passes *anything*.

Snorting into my wine, I pick up my phone and pull up the meal delivery service. I'm going to enjoy my wine, eat a delicious meal, and not think about him until I have to. Ryan Pierce Westerhaven will have to live with the idea that not everything is up to him anymore. I look forward to going head-to-head with him. I know I'll win. He doesn't have the grit.

HOLD MY HEART

Chapter Four

Ryan

"Is there anything else you need, Mr. Pierce Westerhaven?"

I glance across to where Andy is standing at the door, his phone in one hand, his satchel slung over his shoulder. My eyes dart to the clock on my computer screen. Six-thirty. Shit. I didn't realize how late it has gotten. Rubbing my eyes with my forefinger and thumb, I shake my head.

"No. That's all, Andy. Have a good night."

He nods, closing the door behind him as he leaves. Yawning, I turn back to the computer, clicking on the next document, my eyes scouring the lines of the proposal. The silence swirls around me. I must be one of the last ones here. That's fine by me. I work best at night. My eyes land on the time again. Shit. Snatching up my phone. I send a quick message to cancel my date tonight. She was a bit-part actress in a soap, but she's gorgeous. It would have been a fun night. Too bad I'm not leaving here until I figure out how to best Ms. Hall.

Tossing my phone back onto the desk, I turn my eyes to the computer, ignoring the buzzing protestations of my now-abandoned date. I have bigger fish to fry right now. My eyes linger on the last line of the final proposal. I've read all four now. Groaning, I lean back in my chair, my arms stretched behind my head as I grit my teeth. I hate that they're cohesive, coherent, and make sense.

They're going to work, and that's the most grating thing. I looked at her qualifications. She has a background in management. Plucked from obscurity as a manager at Haven Freight. I have no idea how the fuck she came up with these proposals for pharmaceutical-specific issues. All I know is that I would have come up with something similar – in fact, I have notes for a *very* similar solution, just with a few tweaks, from where I was jotting down ideas for when I got to it. My tweaks would make it better, so she's not perfect.

Grabbing my phone again, I swipe away the notifications. We're not going on a makeup date. There's no reason to respond. I don't dip my toe twice. There's no point. It would just give them ideas and get their hopes up. I might be a playboy, but I'm not a dick. Tapping Timmy's number, I lean back, staring at the ceiling while I wait for him to answer.

"Ryan? What's up?"

"Hey, Timmy. How's the fatherhood life?"

"Exhausting. It's almost eight o'clock. I would have thought you would be on a date."

I snort, rubbing my eyes again. "I wish. I'm stuck at work."

"And you're calling me to commiserate? I left work hours ago."

You know, having a baby really changed Timmy. He was a workaholic, but he knew how to party. Now he can't wait to get home to his wife and son. Fucking pussy.

"I'm calling to ask about one of your managers that Uncle Bill poached and sent my way."

There's a moment of silence at the other end of the phone. "Uncle Bill sent you one of my managers? Why? What would a freight manager know about pharmaceuticals."

I'd like to know the answer to that too. "A fucking lot if the proposals I'm staring at have anything to say about it."

"That's probably why he sent them to you."

"She's overstepping."

Timmy snorts. "So, fire her."

My teeth grind, and I stare belligerently at the last line of the proposal on my screen. "I can't. She's the new COO. Only a consensus by the board or gross professional negligence can get this thorn out of my ass."

"Ouch. Uncle Bill promoted one of my managers to COO of Haven Pharmaceuticals? What, is she a prodigy or something? How did he even find her?"

"Fucked if I know. What can you tell me about Layla Hall when she worked for you?"

HOLD MY HEART

"Uh... nothing. I don't know the names of all my managers. Why would I? Do you know the names of yours?"

I rack my brains. Fuck. No. I don't. "Point taken. She's good, whoever she is."

"So, prove you're better."

"Oh, I will. Thanks, Timmy. Enjoy the night shift."

"Fuck off, prick."

Chuckling, I hang up, dropping the phone again. Scrubbing my face with my palms, I hit "track changes" and scroll back to the top of the document. I'm not going home until I have adjusted these proposals for all the changes I flagged. As I said, Layla Hall isn't perfect. I intend to point out every flaw, flag it, and improve on it. I'm not letting weaknesses through my systems. I don't care if I'm here all night.

Layla

Stepping off the bus, I take a deep breath, sling my purse over my shoulder, and walk down the street to the wide glass front doors of the sprawling Haven Pharmaceuticals building. I smile as my eyes drift over the building's outline. I never thought much about the facilities I have worked in, but this one is spectacular.

Haven Freight was in a large, sprawling sandstone building. In Chicago, when I was there for my extended interview, Haven Enterprises was in one of Chicago's distinctive stone skyscrapers. Haven Pharmaceuticals is very LA. It's four levels of glass and steel, glinting in the sunshine with leafy green trees out the front, erupting out of sprawling lawns.

The huge front doors whir open, and I step into the cool interior, my heels clacking on the polished marble flooring. The high ceilings of the atrium rise above me as I cross the room, scanning my card through the security line over the side and stepping into a filling elevator.

"Good morning, Ms. Hall." One of the technicians flashes me a smile as I stand beside her.

"Good morning, Riley."

I have always had an eye for faces, which has been useful in my new position. I have most of the employees' names memorized and cataloged to faces. Riley's face lights up, like my remembering her name has made her day. *That's* why I'm so thankful for my weird skill set. The elevator slowly clears out on each floor until only I remain by the time it reaches the fourth. With a ding, the doors slide open, and I walk out, breezing through the hallways, stepping into my office, and flashing Karly a smile as she rises from her desk, clutching two iced coffees.

"Good morning, Ms. Hall!"

"Hi, Karly! Come on through!"

She hurriedly trails me into my office as I drop my purse onto the desk, sinking into my comfortable leather chair and beaming as Karly sets my iced coffee in front of me.

"No meetings this morning," Karly announces, dropping into the chair across the desk, sipping her coffee as she balances her iPad on her knee, tapping around with her spare hand.

"Good. I caught a glimpse of my inbox." I grimace as Karly giggles. I'm not kidding. I had at least 200 emails that weren't there yesterday. Who knew being COO meant a million emails a day?

"So, no disturbances this morning?" Karly guesses, tapping her iPad to make a note. She knows me so well. Smirking, I snatch up my iced coffee, savoring the taste as I sit back in my chair, waggling my eyebrows at her. Karly giggles, setting her iPad on the edge of the desk and settling back into her seat.

"So, you met Mr. Pierce Westerhaven."

"And survived," I brag, crossing my legs at the knee, surveying the room like a queen. Karly shakes her head, making a face.

"You're a braver woman than me. I was quaking in my heels, and he wasn't even mad at *me*!"

I wave my hand dismissively. "There's nothing to be scared of. He's like any bully, deflating the second someone stands up to him. If he ever comes at you, you let me know. I'll happily take him down a peg or two."

"I want to be you when I grow up," Karly sighs dreamily, collecting her iced coffee and iPad as she stands, closing the glass door behind her and moving to her desk to get back to work. Smiling, I take another sip of my iced coffee, setting it aside as I turn on my computer, tapping my fresh nails on the wooden desk as I wait for it to boot up and my emails to load.

I bite back a sigh at the sight of my full inbox. It was so pretty and under control when I left last night. The first few are memos, so they're easy to clear out. I scan through a few more, finding my rhythm as I answer them.

After about an hour, with new emails constantly coming in, I almost have them under control. The next one catches my eye. It's from Ryan, sent late last night. What the hell was he doing sending an email at almost midnight? Did he get back from a date with some supermodel and have a demand to make? Clicking on it, I scan the words. I'm cc'd in, and so are

HOLD MY HEART

Mr. Westerhaven and the board. My breath is cold in my nostrils, and my heartbeat is loud in my ears.

"What the *fuck*?" I screech, gaping at the screen as Karly bursts into the room, clinging to the door so she doesn't trip in her high heels, her eyes wide.

"Ms. Hall? Layla? What's wrong?"

I mouth wordlessly like a fish, pointing ineffectually at my computer screen.

"He… he…." I get out, my tone faint and my words fading to nothing. Karly hesitantly steps away from the door, apprehensively rounding my desk, her eyes tight as they land on the screen. When she doesn't see an awful visual or whatever she's picturing, Karly relaxes, leaning over my shoulder to read the text on the screen.

"Mr. Pierce Westerhaven sent you an email proposal?" she guesses, completely confused. Yeah. He has. The *bastard*!

"Not just *any* proposal." I poke at the screen again. "He has sent a very well-put-together proposal. For the four issues *I* was hired to implement *my* changes for."

"Oh. That's a dick move." Karly straightens, wrinkling her nose.

"Yeah. It is."

She jumps back as I shove out of my chair, snatching my phone out of my purse, tapping around to bring up the proposal email, and storming out of the room. Karly watches me go with wide eyes but doesn't follow. Good. This is between Ryan and me. We don't need an audience.

"Ms. Hall?" Andy, Ryan's assistant, leaps to his feet as I shove my way into the outer office.

"Where is he?" I spit out, brandishing my phone at the glazed glass wall.

"Uh, he's in his office, ma'am."

Good. Throwing Andy a glare to warn him to stay the hell out of this, I march over, propelling the glass door open, and stalk inside. Ryan lifts his dirty blond head as I stomp inside, knocking the door shut with my elbow. He smirks over at me, lounging back in his leather desk chair, an elbow resting on the arm, his finger brushing his stubbled chin as one dark eyebrow quirks. Ugh. How *dare* he look yummy right now? That shouldn't be allowed. He's a dick. He should look like a horse's ass. Which he *is*!

I stop in front of his desk, one hand landing on my hip as I brandish my phone across the desk at him. "What is this?"

He blinks innocently. "What is what? Your phone?"

Oh, don't pull that "I don't know what's happening" shit with me! I pull up the email, dumping the phone on the desk in front of him and jabbing my finger at it.

"This!"

Ryan leans forward over his desk to peer at my phone. His eyes dart over the email. After a moment, he leans back in his chair, smirking at me. "You mean my proposal for certain issues bookmarked in my emails?"

What the hell is he trying to say? Does he honestly think I hacked into his emails or something? My cheeks flame at the implication in his tone. How *dare* he imply that about me? Besides, we're losing sight of the most important point right now. Straightening, I mash my lips together, crossing my arms over my chest as I glare down at him. My tone is snippier than I intended, but it gets my point across.

"They already have solutions. They don't need a proposal."

Ryan's smug smirk is back, his fingers steepling in front of his chest as he looks up at me with those stupid bright blue eyes. Ugh.

"Maybe I think these are better than the current floated solutions."

My mouth drops open. I shouldn't let him get to me, but I can't help it. He may be the most infuriating human being ever to grace this earth. I snatch my phone up, clutching it to my chest as I shoot daggers at him from my eyes.

"They're not floated. They're board approved."

"Maybe not after the board votes on these." A grin tugs at the corners of Ryan's lips, and he gestures at his door. "I'm sure you can agree that they're an improvement on your initial suggestions."

"Board-approved solutions," I snap back. "And I'm sure yours add *nothing*."

"We shall see, won't we, Ms. Hall?"

"We shall, Mr. Pierce Westerhaven."

His grin falters the slightest bit. "I've told you, Layla, it's Ryan."

Ah, I guess I hit a nerve. Offering him a bloodless smile, I spin on my heel, stalking out of the room. I need to read his proposals before the board meeting to discuss them. I need to be able to shoot them down. And I need more coffee. Stat.

Chapter Five

Layla

"Ms. Hall," Andy murmurs apologetically as I storm out of Ryan's office. I barely spare him a glance. He's the enemy right now, even if he doesn't deserve that label. I stomp my way back along the length of the building to my office, where Karly is waiting with a fresh iced coffee.

"You're a mind reader," I sigh, my step losing some of its anger as I take the drink from her, moving into my office. Karly follows me with a wry smile.

"I saw the board meeting invite pop up in your calendar for this afternoon. I figured you'd need sustenance to study up on his proposal. There's a bear claw on your desk."

I definitely picked the right PA. "Thanks, Karly. You're an angel."

She shrugs, her hand resting on the door handle as she leaves. "I'll hold all calls and make sure you're not disturbed."

The glass door closes quietly behind her as I nod, dropping into my chair and staring belligerently at my computer screen, where the offending proposal is still open. Ugh. What a dick.

Slumping back in my chair, I suck down some icy coffee, my eyes lingering on the lovely print of the LA skyline I sourced. I can't see the skyline from out the window here – though my leafy green view is gorgeous – so I got this one to remind me I made it here. I'm the COO of this damn company, and I got the job based completely on merit. I'll show that... that... *Westerhaven*!

I put down my iced coffee, pulling the keyboard closer to me as I split the screen, setting Ryan's proposal on one side and bringing up a blank document on the other. I have all morning to go through his proposal with a fine-tooth comb and write a report detailing why my solutions are more effective and just plain better.

As I furiously type, my nails clack over the keyboard, the sound spurring me on in the otherwise silent room. Ryan might have had longer in this industry than me, but I've been over these issues and my solutions so many times. I know they're good. I had to defend them to the board and Mr. Westerhaven to get them approved. There are no holes. They are watertight.

My eyes dart to the door as it creaks open, but Karly doesn't speak as she tiptoes into the room, flashing me a smile and setting down a chai latte and a salad wrap. Oh. My eyes land on the computer clock. Lunch. Shoot.

Hold My Heart

"Thanks, Karly." I flash a smile, absently reaching out to pick at my wrap as I keep typing. I need to get this sent off in the next hour. The board meeting is in three, and I want everyone to have time to, at the very least, skim-read my report before the meeting.

My chai latte is empty, and only a few crumbs and a shred of lettuce remain of my wrap when I reply to Ryan's email, cc'ing Mr. Westerhaven and the board in as I attach my rebuttal report and add it as an item of business in the upcoming meeting. Grim satisfaction surges through me, and I sit back in my chair, smiling to myself, my eyes finding the LA skyline again. I watch my emails, but no responses roll in. Maybe he's so cocky he won't even read it. Probably. That seems like it would be in character.

Well. More fool him. I made excellent points in my rebuttal report, and if he's going into the board meeting without reading it, he will go in unarmed and look like a fool in front of everyone.

I look forward to seeing that.

Ryan

I glance at my watch as I stride along the hallway. The board meeting starts in half an hour. I'm not the first to arrive. Andy has been here for an hour, setting up the room, making sure the coffee machine in the corner is ready, the snack table is stocked, and there is fresh water and glasses at every seat. He also has laid out an iPad at every spot, with my proposal front and center.

"Mr. Pierce Westerhaven." He nods to me as he straightens, fidgeting with his tie. It's a nervous tic he has. The man would be terrible at playing poker. Everyone knows it. Some of the technicians have a weekly game. They keep inviting him, but he took my advice to stay away from the game if he wanted to save all his money.

"Thanks, Andy. You've loaded Ms. Hall's report too?"

"Yes, sir. It's the item of business immediately following yours. They simply swipe to turn the page, and her report will show."

He demonstrates to me, turning as someone steps into the room.

"Mr. Keller, can I get you a coffee?"

"Thank you. Ah! Ryan." Lucas Keller claps me on the shoulder, flashing a bright white grin. "I see you and our new COO have already started competing."

Hold My Heart

Turning to him, I grin, shoving my hands into my pockets. Lucas was the CEO before Uncle Bill deemed me ready to hand over. He's a mentor to me and agreed to stay on in his retirement as Chairman of the Board.

"Friendly fire," I assure him. Lucas smiles, accepting his coffee from Andy and taking his seat at the foot of the table.

"She certainly seems like she can hold her own." Lucas's voice is full of admiration. I smirk, taking my seat at the head of the table. I read her rebuttal report. I have my responses prepared, but I can respect the hell out of her not backing down and getting it done so quickly after storming out of my office this morning. While I may feel some grudging respect for my pixie-like, prissy nemesis, that doesn't mean I will go easy on her. If anything, I intend to double down. I love a challenge, and Ms. Hall has presented me with one like I haven't encountered in a while.

I'm enjoying myself. It will be an accomplishment when I run her out of the company and out of town. Hell. I'll even magnanimously request Timmy give her a job back in San Diego. And not a run-of-the-mill manager either. She can head a team there. The rest of the board file in, accepting coffees from Andy, nodding to me, and taking their seats. When Ms. Hall walks in, there are several grins. I have no idea if it bodes well for me, but I hope it does.

I give her a stiff, cursory nod as she takes her seat to Lucas's left. She is dressed in the same outfit as when she barged into my office this morning – a high-necked, long-sleeved top with double buttons that wouldn't look out of place on a marching band leader, paired with a form-fitting pencil skirt and heeled pumps.

I very much enjoyed watching her stomp out of my office this morning. Her skirt displayed every jolt of her ass as she went. The only change is that her hair, which was flowing freely this morning, has been pulled back into a ponytail. I preferred it loose. She was like an avenging Amazon.

All faces turn to Lucas as he clears his throat. "Thank you all for joining us here today. We have an apology from Helen Lawlor, and Andrew Henning is joining by invitation to take notes."

He quickly runs through the quorum, and the schedule, noting Ms. Hall's additional item. She looks smug, but I'm ready for her. Finally, Lucas turns to me with an open-palmed gesture.

"Ryan, if you would care to begin your presentation."

Standing, I button my suit jacket, offering a smile as I take the clicker Andy hands me, moving to stand beside the TV screen where my proposal presentation is loaded.

"As you all know, Haven Pharmaceuticals has been facing industry-wide issues in four key areas. Manual inventory management, the need for faster, more accurate, and transparent operations, supply chain management, and better data analysis for product performance."

As I speak, my eyes sweep the table. There are more nods, some small smiles, and a *lot* of eye contact. They definitely agree with me. My eyes meet Ms. Hall's, which are tight, her mouth mashed into a thin line. I can think of more things her generous lips could be doing than pursing in disagreement, but that's a thought for another time.

Shifting my stance, I put on the hard sell; the *why* of why the board should adopt my changes to Ms. Hall's proposals. I keep it clean. I ensure I don't knock her as a person and don't obnoxiously point out that she has been in this industry for less than a month. Both would cost me goodwill, and I'm not an idiot.

Flashing a smile, I make my closing arguments. "Ms. Hall's proposals were good. They were well-thought-out. However, I'm sure you can all see with these additional changes, Haven Pharmaceuticals would be better placed to be a market leader in these issues, at less of a cost to our bottom line."

Ms. Hall's smile is almost brittle as she returns Lucas's nod, shoving to her feet and approaching me. With a grin, I hand over the clicker, our fingers brushing as she takes it. My skin tingles where she touches me. Ha! She knows I've got her. She must have been sitting there, shuffling her feet back and forth on the area rug in her nervousness, building up static energy.

Flexing my hand, I sit, swinging the chair around to watch her rebuttal presentation. Ms. Hall's hand holding the clicker shakes slightly – I've got her. This is in the bag – but she manages a warm smile, looking around the table to make eye contact. She reaches my eyes last, and the warmth has definitely cooled.

"Thank you all for the opportunity to defend my solutions. I've stood before you once to do this, and, as Mr. Pierce Westerhaven was not present, I understand his need to question my ideas."

Ryan. It's Ryan. How many times do I have to tell her that? Being called *Mr. Pierce Westerhaven* by a direct colleague makes me feel a million years old and a prick to boot. Of course she had to defend her ideas to the board before they originally signed off on them. I would expect nothing less. Hell, *I* have to defend ideas to the board. That's the whole point of a god-damn board.

My teeth grind as she attempts to shoot down my changes. As I'm seated at the head of the table, facing in the other direction, I can't check how her presentation is being received without being a complete asshole, spinning in my chair to make eye contact with fellow board members. Instead, I steeple my fingers in front of my mouth, watching her carefully, hoping my annoyance at going through this charade doesn't show.

"Thank you for your consideration. If you have any questions regarding anything I have put forward, I welcome them."

Ms. Hall flashes a smile, setting the clicker beside Andy as she walks back to her seat, sinking into it, and taking a deep breath. I hate that she did well. That's irritating.

"Thank you, Layla," Lucas flashes her a smile, drawing the table's attention to himself. "Does anyone require clarification on either Ryan or Layla's positions?"

A few queries are thrown out there, and Ms. Hall is poised with her responses. I have to admit another grudging respect for that. She came prepared despite the short notice of this meeting. I'll give her that.

Finally, Lucas clears his throat. "Well, given the need for further clarification on those few items, shall we vote on items one and two of the proposals? Inventory management and field operations?"

Around the table, murmurs of assent sound out. Perfect. Lucas checks his iPad again, drumming his fingers. He taps around to bring up the voting software and grins around the table.

"If you could all input your votes for whether you wish to stick with the current proposals submitted by Layla or implement the changes Ryan has suggested. Make sure you hit submit on both, and I can announce the results for the record."

There is a shuffling as everyone moves in their seat, reaching for their iPads to submit their votes. Leaning forward, I pick up my iPad, tap into the voting section, and select the boxes for changing to my solutions. Hitting the green submit button, I set the device back on the mahogany hardwood of the table, polished so I can see my face reflected in it.

Around the table, most are setting their iPads back down, a few dithering with frowns. I fight to keep my brow smooth and my face neutral. I blew her suggestions out of the water. What is there to dither about?

Lucas nods, his eyes fixed on his iPad as the results come through. Finally, Michael Espinoza taps the submit button, sitting back in his chair, and Lucas looks up. His eyes meet mine, something I don't like flashing through them before he addresses the table.

"For item one, the board has voted five four to continue with the current solution being implemented, and for item two, the vote is six three to continue. No changes will be implemented at this time."

Hold My Heart

Fucking *what*? I keep my face neutral, though I don't miss the small triumphant smile that crosses Ms. Hall's before she swallows it. Lucas wraps up the board meeting, but my mind is racing. I shake a few hands, listening to meaningless explanations of why people voted against my changes. They all seem to stem from the fact that Ms. Hall's solutions have already started implementation. Never mind that my changes wouldn't affect *any* work that has already occurred.

I follow the crowd out of the room, waving off Lucas's suggestion of a drink. I don't have time for a drink. I need to be sharp. I need to write reports on items three and four to cover the questions that arose during the discussion part of the meeting. I glare at the back of Ms. Hall's head, but she doesn't look around, moving off with Michael Espinoza and Georgia Frederickson.

Stepping into my office, I flex my hands but fight the urge to shout or rage as Andy steps in behind me, closing the door.

"Mr. Pierce Westerhaven?"

I glance around at him, sighing and rubbing my eyes with my forefinger and thumb.

"Andy. Bring up my diary. Both work and personal. I want to see everything I have coming up for the next month."

"Yes, sir." Andy fumbles his iPad open, holding it up and running through my packed schedule. There is nothing out of the ordinary, and I let the names and dates wash over me.

I need to be ruthless. I need to throw my whole being into fighting back control of my company from this woman who has apparently bewitched *everyone* at Haven Pharmaceuticals.

"Cancel it all."

"S-sir?"

I turn to where Andy is staring at me, confusion splashed across his face, his fingers hovering over the device screen. Gesturing to the iPad in his hands, I frown.

"Cancel every personal thing in my life. Dates, parties, everything. I need to focus. No distractions. It doesn't enter my radar if it's not pertinent to Haven Pharmaceuticals. Clear?"

"Yes, sir. Uh, you have a date tomorrow night. The Victoria's Secret model, Di -."

"What part of everything means don't cancel dates? Cancel it. There will always be more models. This may be my only chance to oust Ms. Hall."

Andy nods, hurrying out of the room as I stalk over to my desk, dropping into my chair and glaring at the screen. Opening my proposal, I delete the first two items. That's a lost cause. I need to find every hole in items three and four, tearing them apart. This means war.

Chapter Six

Ryan

My fingers flex to avoid drumming them on the table as the final members cast their votes. I have thrown everything into this. I'm so fucking confident that my proposal for item three is the better option for the board. Lucas's eyebrows pull together as the final vote is cast. He looks up with a pained sigh.

"Five all."

Fuck.

"Let's talk this through again. What would cause anyone to move either way?"

Greta Hawthorne shifts in her seat. "I like the new proposal. But I think we should keep some elements of the original proposal."

They want to split the difference. Are you kidding me?

Michael Espinoza pipes up, nodding. "I agree. The less centralized warehouses would work well with the new proposal to run surveys to ensure we're stocking the goods required in that area specifically."

Murmurs go around the room as Lucas nods, typing the new combined proposal into the voting system. My teeth grind as I look down, tapping on the item and reading the combined proposal. This is such fucking bullshit. It's the best option to solve the problem, so I hold my nose and vote for the damn thing. The voting occurs faster than the last three rounds, with everyone casting their votes within minutes. I have no idea if that bodes well for the proposal or not. Then again, I'm officially unsure of everything from here on out. Ms. Hall has managed to blindside me whenever I am confident in something.

"Unanimous," Lucas announces. Fucking bullshit.

I smile along with everyone else, seething inside. My eyes land on Ms. Hall's face, my teething grinding at the smirk there. Her eyes meet mine. Yeah, it's a smirk. It might be irrational, but I'm pissed off that she's happy with this result. That she thinks this is her getting one over me. Only a few parts of her original proposal have been kept. The majority is *my* proposal, some parts of which are polar opposites of her suggestions. She should be more annoyed that the board has aligned with the majority of my recommendation.

Of course, the few parts of her proposal that have been kept happen to be some of the most important aspects of the solution. Fuck. No wonder she's so smug.

"Thank you all. We'll see you back here in three weeks for the next meeting. We'll also vote on the final section of Ryan and Layla's proposals. If you two could have your detailed reports sent around for perusal on the Monday before the meeting at the latest."

I stand as everyone does, keeping time with Lucas as we stride out. He follows me into my office, grinning as he closes the door, sinking into the couch, and accepting the glass of whiskey I hand him.

"You're annoyed at the joint solution," he guesses shrewdly. Sighing, I slug back the whiskey and drop onto the couch across from him, shrugging.

"I think my solution was the better option, unmolested."

Lucas carefully studies me, setting his ankle on his knee, resting his wrist on his bent leg, and clutching his tumbler. I am about to start squirming under his scrutiny when he squints at me.

"Do you truly believe that?"

I hesitate. Do I? Mirroring his seated posture, I drum my fingers against my ankle, thinking through the new, adjusted solution. My breath hisses between my teeth.

"No. The joint solution is the best option for the company."

Lucas smirks as he takes a deep drink of his whiskey. "How did that taste coming out of your mouth?"

"Bitter as fuck," I spit out, sipping my whiskey to banish the phantom taste of bile. I'm not kidding. I hated saying that. Admitting it. Admitting that my idea could be improved. It's a hard pill to swallow. I've been so used to being the brilliant, young board member with all the fantastic ideas. Now Ms. Hall has come along... younger than me, with no background in pharmaceuticals and no experience in the industry, and she can improve upon my ideas? It's hard to take.

Lucas smiles, draining his whiskey and standing, setting the glass on my desk. He turns to me as he reaches the door, pointing a finger in my direction. "A little healthy competition might be just what the doctor ordered. You were getting bored. Admit it. Layla is perfect for challenging you. You thrive under pressure."

"Maybe," I grumble, unwilling to admit he's right... again. With a chuckle, Lucas leaves, pulling the glass door shut behind him. Sighing, I cross the room, leaving my tumbler beside his for Andy to collect, rounding the desk, and sinking into my chair. I'm about to read through the combined proposal that Ms. Hall has just emailed through – she got that done fast, probably enjoying digging her heel into my chest that her ideas were included – when my video chat icon starts ringing. David.

I click on it immediately, a grin crossing my lips as David's tired face shows up in a hospital room.

"David! Where are the twins?"

HOLD MY HEART

Chuckling, he eagerly turns the camera around, panning to where Ani is lying in a bed, two small blanket-wrapped babies in her arms.

"Andrew and Leah," David announces, pride seeping through his voice. As he moves the camera nearer, I get a close-up of each tiny, scrunched-up red face.

"They're gorgeous! Well done, Ani!"

She smiles tiredly at me, mouthing a kiss, while David whines in the background.

"Ani? I helped!"

"You got laid eight months ago. Congratulations," I drawl, drawing a giggle from Ani, who nods vigorously in agreement with my assessment.

"Fuck off, cunt," David laughs. Ani makes a face at him – probably admonishing him for swearing in front of the babies – and the camera flips back to David's face.

"Am I the first one to meet them?"

He rolls his eyes, flipping off the phone. "Nope. We called Timmy before, and Ani's mom has been staying with us for the last month. Mom flew in last week, and Dad is in the air now on his way here."

"Rude. I'm your favorite cousin. I should have been first."

"Keep dreaming."

"Whatever. You'll see when we're all in Chicago for Dad's birthday. I'll be their favorite uncle. Timmy can suck on that."

Laughing, David ends the call to chat with Max and Beau to share the news. I reach for my whiskey tumbler, ready to drink to Andrew and Leah's health, when my eyes land on Ms. Hall's email again, my fingers freezing inches from the glass. Her smug smirk floats through my mind, and I leave the tumbler where it is, clicking on the email attachment instead, loosening my tie as I sit back in my chair, reading through the proposal. It's better than either of us came up with on our own, and I fucking hate that fact.

Layla

Sliding the key into my bright red and white front door, I turn at my squealed name. Karly steps out of the cab, knocking the door shut with her hip as she hurries over, brandishing a bottle of wine. I laugh, holding the door open for her to follow me inside. We both kick off our stilettos, leaving our purses on the sideboard beside the stairs as Karly sinks into one of the squashy gray overstuffed armchairs, and I pad through to the kitchen in search of two wine glasses.

Karly already has the wine bottle open when I reappear in the living area, setting the glasses down on the reflective black glass coffee table with gold trimmings. As soon as mine is full, I pluck it up, sit on the matching squashy couch, tucking my stockinged feet underneath me, and take a sip. Karly shoves her glasses up her nose, her bright red corkscrew curls now loose from the bun she was wearing at the office. She must have taken the pins out in the taxi. She waves her hand around as she takes a sip of her wine.

"That was a win for us, right?"

"Yeah." I sigh, take a slug of wine, and rub my forehead. Karly's grin falters, and she frowns.

"But..?"

"He's such an ass!" I rage. Karly catches her smile, tucking her feet under her to match my posture, slowing drinking her wine, and waiting for me to expand. Does it need to be expanded? Ugh!

"My proposal was better. 100% better. Smaller, decentralized warehouses are the *best* way to solve the crippling supply chain issues. It will give Haven Pharmaceuticals an edge over the competition because we can get the goods to the pharmacy faster than anyone else."

"So why did the board like his proposal?"

I make a face. Money. That's why. "Most of his proposals revolved around carrying high demand stock specific to an area."

"Isn't that a good thing for the company?" Karly asks, frowning as she tries to determine why I'm annoyed at his arguments.

"Yeah. It is."

"So... it's good that the board split the difference?"

"Yes," I grit out, my teeth grinding. Karly giggles, rolling her eyes at me.

"Do you hate that he got that part right and you missed it?"

"Yes."

"Breathe. You'll chip a tooth talking like that."

I'm itching to throw a pillow at her, but that red wine would stain my lovely gray armchair. I settle for poking my tongue out, and she responds in kind.

"Maybe the board only gave that to Mr. Pierce Westerhaven to keep him happy?"

I'd love it if that were even remotely true... but it's not. It was a good idea. I can't believe I missed it in my proposal. I'm so annoyed at myself that I missed it. It's, like, the most obvious thing in the world. I can tell Karly is only saying it to make me feel better. There's no way she thinks the board would pander to Ryan like that. Not when they didn't for the first two proposals.

"I think I'm going to have to change my line of attack," I sigh, taking another sip. Karly's thick, dark eyebrows shoot up, her bright blue eyes wide.

"Why is that?"

"Because I'm starting to understand that Ryan isn't just around because he's a Westerhaven. He knows his stuff." I blow out a breath, tucking a loose strand of hair behind my ear.

He really does know his stuff. Which only serves to make him even more irritating. Somehow, I liked it better when I thought he was just a gorgeous piece of walking nepotism that I could easily best. Him having a brain and knowing how to use it will make my life harder, especially when I'm determined to win at any cost. He still got his job because of his last name. I need to remember that. I'll show him.

Chapter Seven

Ryan

My eyes dart back over the last paragraph I have written on my proposal for the final issue Ms. Hall has "solved," the data analysis for stock movements and sales analytics. Even I have to admit that introducing an internal RFID is inspired. It makes sense that she would use RFID in her solution. Haven Freight uses internal RFID on everything, and she's come directly from working in that system.

Haven Pharmaceuticals is already implementing RFID tracking as part of Ms. Hall's solution to the expensive, time-consuming issue of annual inventory counts. Or, as I like to think of it, Issue One. I am actually in agreement with part of her proposal for this last issue, which is to use that RFID system to track the volume of drugs leaving the warehouses and feed into an automated system to track which items are most profitable.

I don't agree with her suggesting we set up the internal system. This is highly confidential data. Our competitors would kill to get their hands on it. We need to keep it high level, and the method she suggests is too convoluted. Smirking, I start to type out my conclusion when my email pings. My eyes drift over to the other side of my screen to read the memo one of the senior project managers has sent through. I click on it, my lips pressing together. Well, that's just stupid.

Reaching for my desk phone, I punch in the internal line connection for the manager, drumming my fingers on the desk as I frown at the computer screen.

"This is Colleen Jackson."

"Colleen, this is Ryan Pierce Westerhaven."

"Oh. M-Mr. Pierce Westerhaven. What can I help you with?" She sounds nervous. She shouldn't be.

"I just got your memo about streamlining the chain of command."

"Y-yes, sir. Ms. Hall has issued all senior project managers with hiring instructions. My team has twenty-eight technicians. So, under Ms. Hall's instructions, I am to hire four junior managers."

"External hires?"

"Well, yes, sir. That's what her instructions said."

"I need you to hold off on any hiring. I'll contact HR and have them pass the message to senior project managers."

"Of course, sir. And the movement to a smaller team structure?"

"Move forward with that. I trust that you will be able to select four members of your current team who can be placeholder junior managers. Assure them they will receive additional compensation while taking on extra duties."

"Yes, sir."

"Someone will be in contact about when we will move forward with any new hiring. The board of directors will need to vote on the hiring changes separately."

Ending the call, I save my proposal, drafting an email to HR, all senior project managers, and Ms. Hall, informing them of the hiring freeze and the use of internal staff to fill the gap. I also draft an email to the board to change the upcoming meeting from discussing Issue Four to circling back to Issue Two to discuss hiring so many new junior managers. The spike in payroll alone would be enormous, and we would need to make cuts elsewhere to cover it. It hasn't been budgeted for, and the board needs to approve such an outlay of expenses. Outside hiring wasn't in Ms. Hall's original proposal. I wonder why she thought it would be a good idea.

Having sent my emails, I open my proposal for Issue Four again, smirking as I keep typing. Maybe they should have voted for my solutions for that issue in the first place. Outside hiring? The woman is insane. The board will never approve that budget.

Maybe I should suggest such an idea without floating it before the board is enough of a lapse of judgment to question Ms. Hall's qualifications for the job. I could kill two birds with one stone... getting my proposal implemented and getting the stone in my shoe that is Ms. Hall out of my life for good. Wouldn't that be a sweet idea?

Layla

Clutching my purse to my chest, I flash the bouncer a grin, following Karly into the nightclub as she keeps a tight grip on my hand, dragging me along. We didn't have to wait long in line – I think Karly might have flashed some of the cash that I gave her – and I'm thankful. I'm wearing sky-high stilettos, and if we had to stand there for too long, I think my aching feet would have forced me home.

Karly drags me past the coat check area – we didn't bring coats – and into the huge main room. Thankfully, she pauses at the threshold so my wide eyes can take everything in. Oh my gosh. This place is *amazing*! The ceiling is miles above us – okay, it's probably only double or triple height, but still – and the multitude of spotlights are changing color as they move across the heaving crowd, leaping and swaying to the music pumping out of the huge speakers, controlled by the DJ up on the stage, spinning tracks.

Several dancers in matching outfits shake their shit on elevated platforms, and waitresses with trays move through the space with consummate skill.

"Come on!" Karly yells into my ear, seizing my hand again to drag me down the steps into the masses. We squeeze our way through, angling to the left rather than the right, where the crowded bar spans the length of the room. She seems to know where she's going, so I let her tow me along, focusing on not getting squished – Karly and I aren't the tallest people here.

Finally, we pop out of the sweaty crowd, coming to a halt in front of another raised platform – less crowded than the first, with its own bar – the stairs guarded by another bouncer.

"Names, ladies?" he asks in a deep, rumbling voice. Karly giggles, fluttering her lashes. Oh god. Is she going to try to flirt our way into the VIP section? Has she done this before? I've never even tried. Karly isn't the confident flirty type, so I'm intrigued about where this is going.

"There's a table booked for Layla Hall."

I blink in surprise as Karly transforms from a club patron to an efficient PA. Well, damn. The bouncer checks his phone, turning his eyes back to us. "And one of you is Layla Hall?"

Hold My Heart

Oh, shit. I fumble with my purse, extracting my ID and holding it out with a smile. He checks it, hands it back, and moves the rope so we can walk through. Okay. That was seriously cool. I'm important enough to get into the VIP section using my own name. I have officially made it. Karly leads me up the stairs, where another waitress meets us.

"Table for Layla Hall," Karly reiterates, receiving a beaming smile as we are led to a smallish, low round table with a curved black leather booth seat surrounding it like a horseshoe. We slide in as the waitress continues to smile at us.

"Cocktails, ladies?"

I flounder, is there, like, a menu? But confident Karly is back. "Two tequila sunrises, please!"

"Coming right up!"

The waitress's ponytail whirls as she turns, hurrying to the bar to request our drinks. I paw through my purse, but Karly's hand lands on mine. "VIP section! I had to put a credit card down!"

I blink at her. "Am I going to need to take a mortgage out on my condo?"

Rolling her eyes, Karly shoves her glasses up her nose and scrunches it at me. "How much are you planning to drink tonight?"

I shrug, toying with my purse in my lap. "Well, not a lot, but you invited friends, right?"

"Yeah. You told me to. And I made sure to invite my girls. They're not going to spend all your money."

I mean, I trust her. The waitress appears, setting down two red and yellow drinks with little umbrellas with a flourish.

"Two tequila sunrises."

"Thanks! We're expecting three more girls!" Karly shouts over the music, plucking up her drink. The waitress nods, whipping out her phone.

"What are their names? I'll let Mike here and Harvey on the door know so they don't have to wait."

Uh, yeah, girlhood solidarity! Karly grins at the waitress. "Ariel Day, Natasha Manning, and Adelaide Edison."

The waitress disappears after shooting off a text, and Karly types a corresponding message to her friends, shoving her phone back in her purse and turning to me with a beaming smile, tapping her cocktail glass against mine.

I take a sip, enjoying the first taste of orange juice and how the tequila doesn't bite too much afterward. Okay, this was a good choice. I'm normally a boring cocktail order, just an old-fashioned, but I like *this*.

Karly smirks at me, leaning closer. I also lean in to hear her over the thudding bass of the DJ booth. "How is your LA friend-making going?"

Hold My Heart

I screw my nose up. I should never have confided in her that I didn't have the faintest clue how to make girlfriends in a new city. Rolling my eyes, I wave around the booth.

"I asked if you could invite *your* friends to my girl's night. How do you think it's going?"

Karly giggles, shaking her head and sipping her drink before answering. "I thought that might be the case. That's why I invited my college besties. You're going to love them. We all went to UCLA together. They're amazing."

Thank goodness for that. I shrink back in my seat when I realize Karly is studying me with pursed lips. I don't like that look. She's totally going to make me share facts about my life. It's not like I'm *ashamed* of it... I just don't like talking about myself.

"I bet you were the life of the party back in San Diego?"

Ugh. Never. I can't think of anything worse. "God, no. I had friends, but like... some."

"Like..?" Karly sucks on her straw again, her cheeks hollowing out as she waves her hand around in circles, prompting me to continue.

"Like, my college roommate Allison and her bestie Karen."

"Ooh, unfortunate name," Karly winces. Giggling, I take another sip – this is a delicious cocktail.

"Maybe. But she's the sweetest human being alive."

"Are you going to visit them sometime soon?"

"Maybe for Christmas or Thanksgiving. I don't have any vacation time to take."

"Ugh. What's the point of being a COO if you can't take a fabulous vacation whenever you want?"

"Maybe if I was an executive with the surname Westerhaven."

Karly giggles, turning at the sound of squealing. A gorgeous brunette with a set of tits on her to make Aphrodite jealous slides into the booth beside Karly, throwing her arms around her.

"Hey, babe!"

"Ari! Yay!" Karly hugs her back as they both turn to me. "Ari, this is my boss, Layla. Layla, this is Ariel Day."

"Lovely to meet you!" I call over the music as I wave to her. Ariel grins, waving back.

"You too!"

We don't get to say much else before there is more squealing, and another brunette, this one less well-endowed in the chest, with the most gorgeous smile, and a pretty blonde with huge eyes join us, sliding in beside Ariel and me.

"And this is Asha Manning and Addie Edison!" Karly points to them. "My boss, Layla."

Hold My Heart

Addie, the blonde sitting beside me, turns with a friendly grimace. "As I say to Karls when she wants to hang out, no work talk! You guys are the enemy!"

The other four laugh while I stare at them, confused. "I don't understand. You work for a rival pharmaceutical company?"

Addie makes a gagging face. "I'm a freelance illustrator. I mainly work on children's books."

"O...kay?"

Karly laughs, leaning her head against Ariel's shoulder. "Addie's best friend is Josh Burnett from Burnett Pharmaceuticals."

My eyes go wide. Oh. Okay. So, our biggest competitor. Addie giggles, holding up her hands in a surrender position as the waitress approaches to take their orders.

"Just the best friend. Don't shoot the buddy!"

I laugh as they order their drinks, turning back to Asha and Ariel across the table. "Are you guys artists too?"

"I wish!" Asha laughs, shaking her head. "I'm a physical therapist. I work mainly with rehabbing car crash victims."

"And I do social media for a small fashion company," Ariel shrugs, slinging her arm around Karly's shoulders. Okay, that's pretty cool.

"How are the roommates?" Addie asks Ariel, accepting her pink cocktail from the waitress with a huge, toothy smile. Ariel wrinkles her nose.

"Moving out. I'm going to need to find some more."

"Ugh, you have the worst luck with roommates," Addie commiserates while Asha and Karly share a knowing look behind Ariel's head. Okay. There's a story there. I think Ariel might be a bad roommate and scares hers off.

"Anyway, let's talk about fun things. Boys!" Karly shrieks, holding her drink out for everyone to toast. Okay, I haven't had a chance to meet any of those either, but I can't wait to hear their stories! I miss having girlfriends.

Chapter Eight

Layla

Stepping into my office, my eyes find Karly sitting at her desk, typing away. She looks up, flashing a smile as I waggle my eyebrows. "Good morning, Ms. Hall. Your iced coffee and a pastry are waiting on your desk."

I wave my hand dismissively. "Don't you *Ms. Hall* me. I saw you leave the club with that tall glass of water. Spill. I need details. Now!"

Karly shrugs, holding back her smug smile. "He was… nice."

"Oh, I bet he was. He certainly looked like he knew how to… nice."

Giggling, Karly twists one of her corkscrew curls around the tip of her forefinger. "He knew how to… nice. Don't you worry about *that*!"

Smirking at her, I step into my office, set down my bag, and snatch up my iced coffee. Sucking down the deliciously icy nectar, I sink into my chair, turn on my computer and open my emails.

I blink, leaning closer to the screen to ensure my eyes aren't playing tricks on me. What the hell? Why is my email filled with back-and-forth emails between Ryan, the board, the senior project managers, and HR? What the hell is going on? Tapping on the first one in my inbox, I scroll to the bottom, my lips mashing as I read Ryan's initial email. The one putting a freeze on ALL hiring. Excuse me? Did he forget the board voted to approve my small teams and junior managers solution? *Twice*!

Karly's head snaps up when the door swings open, and I storm out. She half raises, but I wave my hand at her to tell her to sit the hell down. This is between Ryan and me. She doesn't follow as I stew the entire way down the hallway. Andy isn't at his desk when I march into the outer office, but that's okay. I'm not here to see him. I shove the opaque glass door into Ryan's office open, stepping inside without knocking.

Both Andy and Ryan glance up from where they are seated on either side of the desk, Andy tapping out notes on the iPad he's holding as Ryan dictates something. My voice finds a steel I never knew I possessed.

"Andy. Give us the room."

His eyes widen, but gratifyingly, he doesn't glance at Ryan for confirmation, just scrambles to his feet, retreating and closing the door firmly behind him. When we are alone, Ryan smirks. I ignore his smug look, squaring my shoulders. I don't care that he's never seen me off-balance like this. I don't care that he can probably see that he's finally getting to me.

Hold My Heart

As I approach, he stands, shoving his hands into the pockets of his suit pants, eyeing me cockily. Ugh. Asshole. I storm right up to him, crowding his personal space. He's so tall, I have to tip my head right back, his chin coming down, his smirk still stretching his full lips. Shoving a manicured fingernail into the center of his hard chest, I sneer at him.

"Who the hell do you think you are? You can't get in the way of a board-backed initiative!"

He doesn't remove my finger from his chest, though it must be digging in. His annoying smirk doesn't even falter as he leans down slightly, his face closer to mine, forcing my fingernail to dig into his chest even further.

"I think you'll find I'm Ryan Pierce Westerhaven."

Ugh. What an *ass*! He needs to be taken down a peg or two, and I'm going to be the one to do it. It will be glorious. I dig my fingernail in deeper, trying to see a wince around his gorgeous blue eyes. They look like the ocean off Santa Monica pier. "You are nothing but an unenlightened bully who can't handle not being the sole king in your kingdom anymore."

A low chuckle rumbles out of Ryan, my cheeks flushing pink at the sound. What the hell? He leans even closer, and as he chuckles, his warm breath brushes over my cheeks. My heart is pounding in my chest as he starts to speak, his voice low and husky.

"I think you'll find I will be a worthy adversary, Ms. Hall. You better get ready for the fight of your life."

My mouth drops open, my cheeks flaming for an entirely different reason now. Forget how yummy he is. Forget his sexy chuckle and how good he smells. *I* better get ready for the fight of my life? We'll see about that!

"Oh, I'll be ready, Mr. Pierce Westerhaven. But will *you* be?" I hiss at him, spinning on my heel and stomping away from his grin.

"It's Ryan," he calls after me, laughter coloring his tone. Ugh. I hate him. I think I actually hate him.

I blow past Andy, who calls out goodbye after me, making my way back to my office. Karly looks up, her eyes wide as I step back inside. "Hold my calls, Karly."

"Are you okay?" she asks, standing and hurrying around her desk as I move through the outer room to my office.

"I'm fine. I need to be alone."

She stumbles to a halt, watching me with concerned eyes as I close the world out, sinking onto one of the couches, pressing my shaking hands to my face and chest. Deep breaths, Layla. Keep it together. Shaking my head, I slump back into the couch, staring at the high ceiling. I am furious. Angrier than I have ever been, and I'm mad at myself more than Ryan.

HOLD MY HEART

We were in an *argument*. We were *fighting*. And my body and brain somehow thought that was the perfect time to notice how good he smelled. What the hell? He's my enemy. He's trying to run me out of this company. Hell, out of this city! I should *not* be obscenely turned on by him.

Ryan

The door swings shut on Ms. Hall's delectable ass. Somehow still as noticeable in her 1950s navy pinafore as it was in her pencil skirt the other day. Silence reigns in the room after she leaves, my blood thudding in my ears as I bend over the desk, placing both hands on it to brace myself. My head lowers, and I take a series of deep breaths.

I almost fucking *kissed* her back there. What the fuck? I blame it on not getting any because I've been so focused on this fucking fight. She's not even my *type*! Buzzing angry pixie couldn't be further from my type if she actively tried. The door swings open. "Mr. Pierce Westerhaven? Is everything okay?"

"Get the fuck out, Andy," I snap without looking up.

"Yes, sir. Buzz me if you need anything."

He closes the door behind him, and I continue my deep breathing. I need to get my head in the game. I can't concentrate on crushing her if all I can think about is the smell of jasmine while she's around.

I can't stand here and wallow like an idiot. Straightening, I move to the windows, tucking my hands back into my trouser pockets as I look out over the leafy green park across the road from this building. I was a freshman in high school when Uncle Bill sat me down and told me I would be attending Duke, studying pharmaceuticals, and taking over the LA company someday.

I was a senior in high school when he called me into the Haven Enterprises office to show me a series of architectural sketches and ask for my input on the building style and location. I suggested this building in this location, and that's where they broke ground. That was the day I knew Uncle Bill was serious about me running the company one day.

After four years at Duke, I came in as a junior executive and learned the ropes from Lucas. I worked my way to where I am. I have no idea of Ms. Hall's background, but I know she didn't work half as hard as I did to be standing in this building. I know she hasn't poured her *life* into this company for the last ten years. Hell, I interned here on college vacations.

Hold My Heart

I have earned the right to instruct the board. I have earned the right to make decisions for this company. It is my life and my legacy. To her, it's just a job. I won't let some little pixie swan in here, implement some changes, and move on to bigger and better things when the urge arises.

The whole playboy image is fun. Dating supermodels is fun. But it's superficial. *This* is my life. No one is going to take that away from me. Ms. Hall poked the wrong bear and is about to find that out.

My email dings and I glance away from the view, moving behind my desk and smirking at the memo. An emergency board meeting this afternoon? Ah, Ms. Hall's appearance has to do with the hiring freeze. I did wonder why I didn't hear from her over the weekend about it. She must have only seen it this morning. Chuckling, I sink into my desk chair, clicking to open the email and scan the contents. It's much as I thought it would be. I'm going to be ready. I hope she will be too.

Chapter Nine

Ryan

Lucas takes the coffee cup off Andy, strolling over to me with a smile. "I haven't been in this building so much since I retired. If I'd known bringing on a COO would be *more* work for me, I wouldn't have voted for it."

My eyebrows shoot up. The board voted on her appointment. *And* voted on her measures? I was away for three fucking weeks. Three weeks! Over Lucas's shoulder, my eyes find Ms. Hall stalking into the room in her pinafore. Even her stiletto heels have that little strap like a schoolgirl's shoes. Who dresses like that? Who looks that *good* dressed like that?

Lucas follows my gaze, attempting to see what has distracted me. He grins as his eyes land on Ms. Hall and claps my shoulder as he moves to his spot at the foot of the table. Lucas taking his seat is everyone's cue that the meeting is about to begin, and there is a flurry of seat-taking. He runs through the quorum and schedule and then glances at Ms. Hall.

"Layla. You called this meeting. You can have the floor."

Hold My Heart

"Thank you, Lucas." She squares her shoulders, lifting her chin and turning to address the table while glaring down at me.

"As you know, this board voted to implement my small teams initiative. Twice."

I steeple my fingers in front of my mouth to cover my smirk at her subtle dig. Game on, Ms. Hall.

"This initiative included the necessity for junior managers, which Haven Pharmaceuticals does not currently employ. Mr. Pierce Westerhaven's hiring freeze is a deliberate measure to sabotage my board-backed initiative."

Her chest is heaving. Shit. She feels emotional about this. It's not personal. It's just business. Everything about Haven Pharmaceuticals is business. That's why it's so successful. Lucas turns to me, his eyebrows rising. I can see the warning there and shake my head subtly. Please. He knows me better than to think I would risk anything about Haven Pharmaceuticals for a personal issue.

Nodding, he gestures toward me. "Ryan. Can you please elaborate on your hiring freeze?"

Dropping my hands, I smile around the table. "As I noted in my emails, Ms. Hall's proposal, either vote, did not include hiring large numbers of personnel to fill her junior management positions. Such a large hiring practice will significantly affect the company's bottom line."

"Where did you think the positions would be filled from?" Ms. Hall blurts out. Lucas pats her arm gently, and she falls silent, glaring at me.

"So, you are saying you wish the board to vote on pausing the small teams initiative entirely until we can get accurate numbers on the underlying cost?"

Oh no. I'm not the bad guy here. I gesture my arms wide. "Not at all. I've already instructed the senior project managers to continue implementing the initiative, selecting existing team members to step up into the junior management positions until we can ascertain whether *any* new staff needs to be hired."

My eyes land on Ms. Hall's face as I continue. "As you all know, it is Haven Pharmaceutical's practice to promote internally wherever possible. I suggest a trial period with the selected staff receiving increased compensation for their elevated roles. After a month, if teams are struggling, we can look at hiring supplemental staff, either at the junior end or the management end if required."

Ms. Hall is chewing her tongue inside her mouth to keep herself quiet. My idea has merit, and she knows it. Yeah, I'm not just a pretty face. Lucas sits back in his seat, drumming his fingers on the table. A few board members throw out some questions. I answer easily, and Ms. Hall answers through

Hold My Heart

gritted teeth. I have so won this round, and she knows it. Success is sweet.

"We'll vote on Ryan's changes to Layla's initiatives. If you will all cast your votes on your iPads."

Casting one last smirk in Ms. Hall's direction, I pluck up my iPad, quickly voting to keep the hiring freeze. All votes are cast within five minutes. Lucas taps his iPad, his gaze darting toward Ms. Hall before returning to the device.

"Unanimous. No new hires for a month until we can assess the internal promotions and their effectiveness."

Unanimous. So even Ms. Hall voted for my changes. She can admit when she has been bested. I have to respect the hell out of that. I catch her eye, offering her a genuine smile. There's no reciprocal look. Instead, she glares icily at me, her fury sparking behind her eyes. Under her hostile gaze, my smile takes on a smug look. It's an automatic response to her antagonism. She doesn't like it. That's okay. She still voted for my measures. I won this round. It's a good feeling. I like winning. I think I like besting Ms. Hall even more.

Layla

I kick off my heels and slam my front door, stomping through the townhouse to collect a glass of wine. I pour it as full as I can without spilling it when it moves and settle myself on my tiny porch. My grass patch looks emerald green, and my fence is a riot of color. Karly organized a fantastic gardening service. They landscaped everything and kept it alive. It's all I can ask. Toying with my phone, I hit Allison's number, waiting for her to answer.

"How's my super-rich bestie?" she squeals down the line. Groaning, I take a large slug of wine.

"Squirreling away every last penny for when I'm a basic broke bitch again."

Allison makes a choking sound, the background music cutting out. She must have turned it down or stepped outside.

"Uh, *why* would you be broke? You're the COO of a billion-dollar company. Bitch, you *are* Big Pharma."

"Maybe not for long." Am I wallowing? You bet your freaking ass I am. What can I say? Ryan Pierce Westerhaven has finally gotten under my skin.

"I thought you said you were loving the work?" Allison is still confused. I don't blame her. I *was* loving the work. I am. I'm just not loving the prick determined to make my life miserable.

HOLD MY HEART

"The CEO is an asshole."

"Ryan Pierce Westerhaven? The only single Westerhaven nephew and renowned playboy? He's an asshole? Really? I would *never* have guessed."

"Cool the sarcasm jets, Janice."

Allison giggles as I sip more wine, already feeling better. My bestie could always cheer me up over the phone.

"So, why is Mr. Rich an asshole?"

Sighing, I drain my wine, staring at my gorgeous garden as I launch into his litany of sins. "He's determined to block all my measures. I'm pretty sure he's hoping I'll get fired for not implementing everything Mr. Westerhaven hired me to do. And he has the *nerve* to look like sex on legs while he does!"

Allison's giggles through the phone are infectious, and I even crack a smile. "So, he's being a thorn in your side when you wish he would be a thorn in your vagina?"

"Ex*cuse* me! No one is putting anything thorny near my vagina!"

"Hey, don't knock it 'til you've tried it!"

"My vagina is a thorn-free zone."

Allison laughs before sighing and focusing on my issue. "Okay. So, he's hot, and you noticed. I'm afraid you can't help that. Cross your legs and keep a spare pair of panties in your office."

Solid advice. Allison isn't finished. "As for the asshole thing.... You should prank him."

"I should... what?"

"Prank him. Park in his space."

"I don't have a car."

"Boo! Bitch, you're a one percenter. Buy a fucking car."

Spare panties in my office, new car.... "These don't sound like saving every penny I can for when I land on your couch without a job."

"Hey, if the car is nice enough, you won't need my couch. You can sleep in it."

"I'm not buying a car. I don't need one. There's a bus."

"Babe, I can't even with you right now. Whatever. Pick a different prank. You're the COO. Have the hallway outside his office repainted so he can't get in until they're finished. Just make his life annoying."

"I don't know how to make someone's life annoying." I know she's being ridiculous, but it's working. My smile is bigger than my face right now.

"Well, lucky for you, I have a big brother. I can coach you through making someone contemplate hiring a hitman."

"You've never thought about hiring a hitman to take out your brother...."

"Have you never wondered why incognito mode is my default browsing function?"

Hold My Heart

O…kay. I have no idea if she's serious or not. I think it's best not to ask.

"I miss you," I sigh down the line. Allison sighs back.

"I miss you too, babe. But you're Little Miss Richie Rich, so *you* have to come back to visit *me*."

"How about around Christmas I pay for us to hit up Cozumel for a few nights?"

Allison sighs dreamily. "I *knew* there was a reason I stuck it out with my annoyingly perfect college roommate. Cozumel sounds heavenly."

"You pick out a resort, and I'll book it. I need some Ali and Layla time."

"Me too. Good luck with your smoking-hot CEO. Keep me posted."

"I will! Love you!"

"Love you more! Byeee!"

Hanging up, I grin at my garden one last time, moving inside to cook a stir fry. Bring it on. I'm going to make Ryan Pierce Westerhaven my bitch. He hasn't seen anything yet!

Chapter Ten

Ryan

Stepping out of my Range Rover Evoque, I toss the keys to the valet and stride up the low-rise stone steps and through the open double glass front doors. I have been to Lucas's Beverly Hills home many times over the years. As usual, he is hosting a cocktail event for the board members. He usually only hosts them a few times a year, and we were here just over two months ago, but with all the impromptu meetings that have been called since Ms. Hall first graced us with her presence, Lucas felt he needed to keep them onside.

"Ryan!" Shirley, Lucas's wife, greets me with an embellished kiss on each cheek. She gestures to a white-jacketed waiter, who presents me with a tray of champagne glasses. I take one with a smile to Shirley, who wags her finger at me.

"You know my rules. Champagne on entry. Then you can guzzle Lucas's whiskey to your heart's content."

Flashing her a grin, I drop another kiss on her upturned cheek, moving into the room to allow Shirley to greet the new arrivals behind me. Classical music pipes through the cream space. The marble tiles on the floor are the same color as the

HOLD MY HEART

walls and ceiling, making the area feel huge and airy. I join Michael Espinoza and Helen Lawlor near the shiny white grand piano, saluting them with my champagne glass.

"Lucas is lucky to have Shirley," Helen notes, looking around at the milling guests and distinct waiters. "She sure knows how to throw a party."

I fix Helen with a skeptical look. "I don't think you need to worry about being outdone in the party aspect. I'm still missing time from when you and Kirsten last hosted."

Helen's cheeks flame and she laughs, pressing her hand against her chest, leaning in conspiratorially. "Kirsten didn't realize she served the cookies with the edibles in them. That was unintentional."

"That was a hell of a party," Michael chips in as Helen giggles. "Talking of a hell of a party."

Michael cranes over my shoulder, nodding toward the door. Helen and I turn to follow his gaze, and I bite back a snort as Ms. Hall walks in. As my eyes drop to her outfit, my eyebrows shoot up. I guess she threw prissy out the window. She's in a tight, one-shouldered cocktail dress that hugs her body down to her ass and flares out to her knees. It's bright red, and it is her *color*.

"Oh, wasn't her townhouse darling?" Helen coos, waving to the new arrival. "I loved her style of having a party to get to know everyone when she started and thanking us for taking a chance on her!"

I sip my champagne to avoid having to speak. Ah, so that's how she got everyone on board. Free booze. It does work wonders. Ms. Hall approaches, clutching her purse and champagne, her smile a little forced. She submits to Helen and Michael's air kisses of greeting and returns my sharp nod.

"Isn't it so nice to all be together and not have to think about budgets and schedules?" Helen laughs, holding her glass in a toast. Michael concurs, and Ms. Hall murmurs something that doesn't quite sound like agreement.

We make small talk about the weather and various events around LA. Eventually, Helen and Michael each drift away, leaving me with Ms. Hall. She turns her gray eyes on me, looking coolly as she sips her champagne. I meet her gaze with a grin. "You want to talk about work."

She shrugs, sipping her drink and tipping her head back to look at me. "I was thinking that everything is running so much more smoothly now we don't have manual inventory counts. You should be thanking me. I've gifted you millions in shareholder dividends."

Grinding my teeth, I keep my smile fixed on my face. "I think you'll find that there were already two quotes Haven Pharmaceuticals had sought over RFID technology for internal stocktake. Your idea wasn't anything special. It's the way the industry was heading. Congratulations on seeing the writing on the internet and putting it in a proposal. Well done, you."

Her mouth drops open in shock as I spin on my heel, walking away. I leave my empty champagne glass on a passing waiter's tray, taking the floating stairs two at a time as I head up in search of an available bathroom. There is one on the lower level, but that's the one everyone will be using, and as I said, I've been here many times over the years. I used to stay here when I interned in high school over the summer vacations.

Slipping into the bedroom that was so often assigned as mine, I don't bother flipping on the lights. Some light is filtering through the window from the lit-up pool area below, and I know where all the furniture is to avoid banging a shin.

Relieving myself, I smirk at my reflection in the mirror. Ms. Hall's face, when I put her in her place downstairs, was a thing of beauty. Those plump pink lips falling open... I could think of a few pleasurable ways to close them. An added benefit of having her lips occupied would be that she couldn't speak.

I step into the bedroom, halting mid-stride as Ms. Hall turns, her petite, lithe figure illuminated at the window.

"Either this room is a homing beacon as a spare bathroom, or you followed me here, Ms. Hall."

She turns her head slightly, her arched eyebrow visible in her backlighting.

"I don't appreciate being spoken to the way I was downstairs," she snipes. Oh good. Her cool tone is back. It will not make her seem like a silver-screen mid-century beauty, so she should just cut the crap.

"Maybe if more people spoke to you that way, you wouldn't have developed such an over-inflated sense of worth."

Her mouth drops open again. I think it's my favorite look on her.

"Over-inflated sense of worth? You think *I* have one of those? Maybe you should go back into that bathroom and take a look in the mirror!" Ms. Hall's tone is almost a screech as she jabs her finger at the doorway behind me. I let a feral grin tug at my lips, taking a step toward her as she holds her ground.

"I know exactly what I look like in the mirror, Ms. Hall. And I know that my sense of worth is inflated to exactly where it needs to be. I have many, *many* people who can attest to that."

She scoffs, rolling her eyes and planting her hands on her hips. "While you're talking about women, I'm talking about work. I earned my position at Haven Pharmaceuticals. Can you honestly say the same?"

HOLD MY HEART

This bullshit again? She's like a fucking broken record.

"Yes, Ms. Hall. I can. You came swanning in this year armed with a wealth of Google knowledge. I've been interning here since I was fifteen. I think we all know who has put in the work. As for my prowess with the ladies, I'm sure you're deflecting because you wouldn't have the first idea how to handle a man like me."

Pressing a hand to her throat, she makes a choking noise, shaking her head as she mouths wordlessly like a guppy. Finally, she finds her words, spitting them out rapid-fire.

"Please, Mr. Pierce Westerhaven. I would hardly consider you a man. An overgrown private schoolboy with an ego he can't handle maybe…."

My breath is cold in my nostrils as I stride toward her, not stopping until our fronts are pressed together. Her head tips back immediately as my hands land on her small hips, my mouth slamming down on hers. I'll fucking show her who is a man.

She is frozen for all two seconds before responding. It's not what I expect – like to be shoved away and slapped – instead, she grips my biceps, her lips parting and her tongue searching for mine, dancing a heated tango when it finds its goal.

"How many times, Ms. Hall," I growl between mauling her mouth and breathing. "It's Ryan."

"Shut up, and kiss me, Ryan," she breathes back, attacking my mouth again. You know, that's one project I'm willing to collaborate on. Still kissing her frantically, I walk her backward until we reach the glossy dresser with the TV mounted on the wall behind it. Layla's fingers scrabble at my belt and fly as I move, managing to get them open. Her hand slides inside, her fingers brushing my eager, aching cock as I tug her skirt up around her waist and lift her onto the top of the dresser, stepping between her spreading thighs.

Layla's hand closes around my tie, holding my head at the angle she wants to kiss me, her other gripping my shoulder through my suit jacket, those perfectly manicured fingernails digging through the fabric, scraping against my flesh. She tastes of mint and champagne, her jasmine scent swirling around me, teasing my nostrils. I can't wait for a second longer. My cock was teased by her light touches, and now the greedy bastard is screaming to be buried balls deep in her, and I intend to oblige. I've denied the poor prick this last month; he deserves this.

Shoving aside her panties, I grip my cock, positioning him at her weeping entrance, and moving my hand to tilt her hips as I slam home, my other hand cupping the back of her neck to continue our heated embrace, our tongues fencing, each attempting to gain dominance.

Hold My Heart

Layla hisses against my mouth as I bury myself in her wet heat, and I hold still, fighting against every urge riding me hard to start thrusting with everything I have. She's so fucking tight, and something occurs to me. Shit. She was wet, but I don't know when she last got laid. I'm here to prove a fucking point, not hurt her.

As I'm about to lift my mouth to ask if she needs a moment to acclimate, Layla's hips start frantically moving, milking my cock. Fuck yeah. That's what I'm talking about. Layla keeps her death grip on my tie, her other hand sliding up from my shoulder to my hair, gripping the short strands tightly. The slight sting of pain is alleviated by our urgent kissing and the vice-like grip her pussy has on my cock as I frantically thrust into her again and again.

Unwilling to be bested in *anything*, Layla's hips match my frenzied rhythm, playing my gratified cock like a banjo at a bluegrass concert.

When I'm worried about doing the most ungentlemanly thing imaginable and blowing my load before she climaxes, Layla's hips lose their tempo, jerking wildly as her pussy flutters, working my cock over. Thank fuck for that. Layla comes hard, unable to keep kissing me as she loses all concentration. She bites down on my lower lip while her pussy clenches my dick. Fuck me. I slam into her, holding fast as I release deep into her heavenly pussy.

My lip is throbbing as she sits back, her bright eyes wide, her pale cheeks flushed beautifully. I withdraw, tucking my cock away and buttoning myself up, still holding her gaze as a satisfied smirk pulls at my lips.

"I guess I was man enough to satisfy you, Layla."

She snaps out of her dreamy state at my words, sliding off the dresser and stepping away from me as she tidies herself up. As her head lifts, she throws me a withering look, a sneer scrunching up her nose.

"I've had better orgasms from my own fingers."

What. The. Fuck? My mouth drops open as she snatches up her purse, brushing past me into the bathroom. The door snaps shut, a line of light appearing on the smooth pine flooring beneath it. What did she fucking say to me? She came *hard*. There's no way her tiny little fingers could satisfy her as much as I just did. My lips press together, and I wince from the slight sting of my lower lip. Shit. I need to ensure my hair isn't too messy and that I don't have teeth marks on my lip before rejoining the party.

Stalking across the hall to the other spare bedroom, I let myself in, flipping on the light. My lip is fine, maybe a little swollen, but nothing noticeable. I carefully smooth my hair, so it doesn't look like Layla was fisting it while I was pounding that sweet pussy. My cock stirs hopefully – the greedy, insatiable prick – and I adjust myself, pausing as I do. Fuck. No condom. What the hell was I thinking?

Layla

Sipping my iced coffee, I settle back on my couch, propping my feet up on the coffee table and staring out of the view. I've just come from a meeting with the senior project managers. Ryan's idea of promoting internally is working well. I can't even be mad about it. It's a good idea to go internal. We know the teams will already work well with people they know and trust. I don't know why I didn't think of it. I guess it's because I didn't want to add more work to people when I heard from a few of them in my meet and greet parties during my first week here that they were feeling stressed.

My eyes flutter closed as I suck down some more iced coffee, my mind wandering. Right into dangerous territory. His hot mouth on mine, his tongue plundering, his dick pounding into me. Shit! I sit bolt upright, surging off the couch and shaking out my limbs. Glaring at the offending, too-comfortable piece of furniture, I stalk over to my desk. It's not as restful, but at least it will not lull me into daydreams of Ryan sex when I came so hard, I saw stars.

Groaning, I shake my head, burying my face in my hands. I lied to him. I've never come that hard before. It was amazing. And so, so stupid. Not only do we work together, but we were also at a work function – so unprofessional – and we didn't use protection – so unbelievably stupid.

I ran to my doctor's the next morning, and I have never felt so relieved when a full STD test panel returned negative. I mean, not that I think he would… argh, whatever. I'm on birth control, but it was still a super dumb thing to do. It won't happen again. I'm sure of it.

We drank champagne – one glass each – and got caught up in the moment. It can't happen again. It's been a week, and I have managed to avoid him successfully. Until now. At least I don't have to be in the same room as him, but I do have to attend the same video conference. We have had the board troop down here so often that Ryan insisted this happen over Zoom. Fine by me. I don't trust myself not to blush if I were in the same room as him. At least this way, I can not look at his little square.

I click on the link in my email, using the test picture to check my hair and makeup. I look fine. I hit enter, waiting in the queue for the meeting to start. In the meantime, I read through Ryan's proposal again. It's not a major issue – hence the online meeting – but it overrides one of my proposals regarding the inventory management system. He needs to back off and stay out of my proposals. They're working. This one is *working*. Has he never heard of the term "if it ain't broke, don't fix it"?! He needs to. Maybe I should have it stitched into a pillow and sent to him as a major freaking hint!

Letting my eyes flutter closed, I take a deep breath. I can't go into this meeting annoyed. That's the best way to ensure Ryan has the upper hand. I refuse to give him an inch. He has to work for it and take it if he wants it. Like I have always had to, every day of my life. I know he said all that stuff about interning here since high school. I would have loved to have been able to have an unpaid internship during my summer vacations, but instead, I served gelato on the beach. Lower middle-class girls with dreams had to hustle, and I did, damn it!

I need to focus on the meeting, not think about the dreams that have consumed me since we screwed, and not think about how irritating Ryan muscling in on my projects is. No. Focus. I will win because my ideas are better. That's all there is to it.

The electronic whooping noise signals the call, and I fix a smile as I appear beside the other board members, including Ryan. I keep my eyes deliberately facing away from his square and make sure I have gallery mode on. I don't want him popping up full screen when I'm not ready because he's talking.

"Thanks for joining us, everyone." Lucas takes charge of the meeting, running through the quorum and housekeeping matters. Finally, Ryan presents his proposal. I squirm in my seat as his warm, rich voice fills the room, but I don't need to worry about my panties getting too drenched because all I have to do is focus on his words for the annoyance to surge through me. Just *who* does he think he is? Yeah, I know. Ryan Pierce Westerhaven. The douchebag.

Unlike previously, I'm not asked to defend the current proposal. Since it has already been implemented, there are reports that can show how well my system is working. I don't think Ryan's suggestion will improve upon it. I don't think it will do anything other than waste time and money.

"If you could enter your votes into the software on your screens," Lucas interrupts my musings.

I don't hesitate to vote to reject his proposal. The other votes come in quickly, thank goodness. I hate waiting. It's nerve-wracking and makes me feel like everyone is watching me to see how I'll react.

"Seven to three to adopt the changes."

Shit. I keep a neutral expression pasted on my face as they conclude the meeting, but I am one of the first to click out of it as soon as it is wrapped up. Snatching up my iced coffee, I dump it in the trashcan under my desk. It doesn't make me feel any better, and now I need more caffeine. Boo. This is all Ryan's fault. Stupid Westerhaven. Stupid, stupid, stupid! He's supposed to be an empty-headed playboy who only got his position based on his family name.

How *dare* he not stick to the script! Even if it irritates me, his proposal wasn't *bad*. I don't think it improved the implemented solution, but it wasn't *dumb*. That makes my mood even worse. He's smart, he's gorgeous, and he knows how to pleasure a woman with that huge dick he's packing in those tailored pants. Life isn't freaking *fair*!

Chapter Eleven

Ryan

Leaning against the edge of my desk, I cross my legs at the ankles, my hands shoved into my pockets, making eye contact with all the managers present, except for one corner of the room. As much as I would love to ignore that corner completely as I run the meeting and guide the team through the logistics of this project, Layla is making it extremely difficult.

She's in another one of her pinafores, a black one this time, over a prissy button-down top up to her chin and frills over her wrists. She should look like a caricature of a nineteenth-century *child*, so why the fuck is my cock hard when I glance in her direction? Her long, dark ponytail flutters around as she moves her head to speak with people, and every time she opens those plump lips it is to shoot down another idea.

This isn't even one of her proposals. I have no idea why she's here, but her name was on the meeting register, and she marched her delectable ass in here and sat it down to make my life hell for the last hour.

Hold My Heart

"As you can see," I continue, jerking my head over my shoulder at the presentation slides illuminated onto the wall behind my desk, "this should increase productivity on the factory floor and cut down on time wastage."

"Wouldn't cultivating a better work/life balance be a more efficient way to increase productivity in the long term? Studies in Europe have shown interesting results in this area," Layla pipes up again, her voice both melodic and grating, all at once. It's quite a feat.

"I think we'll break here. See everyone back in an hour," I bite out. There are a few looks exchanged between some of the managers, but they all duly file out, the door swinging closed behind them. Layla still hasn't moved, tapping notes onto her iPad. Andy sticks his head around the door, but I wave him away, my eyes glued to the top of Layla's head.

"Take lunch, Andy. Be back here in fifty minutes to organize the coffee for the afternoon session."

"Yes, sir."

The door swings shut again, and through it, I can hear Andy collecting his wallet and phone and the wooden door to the outer office clicking shut. When I'm sure we're truly alone, I unleash.

"What the fuck is your problem?"

Layla's head snaps up, her eyes widening in surprise before they narrow, focused on me.

"You are."

My teeth grind together as I glare at her. "Let me reiterate. What the fuck is your problem with the project, exactly?"

Layla rolls her eyes, dropping her iPad onto the coffee table beside her and pointing at the projection behind me. "Yes, some of these measures might save you an ounce of a fraction of a minute per person daily, but those are human beings behind those numbers. There are better ways to get the most out of your workforce, and I don't think a dollar more an hour is it."

"A dollar more an hour is over two thousand dollars more in their pockets a year. You think they don't deserve that?"

"Oh, please," she scoffs, gesturing at me. "How much did your watch cost?"

My hand twitches in my pocket, my watch hidden under my suit sleeve. "It was a gift."

"It was at least five thousand dollars."

Probably more. It was a one-of-a-kind custom gift from my parents for my college graduation.

"What's your point?"

Layla shoves out of her seat, marching toward me. "My point is that I'm sure the company can afford more than a dollar an hour."

I step away from the desk, my hands coming out of my pockets as I advance toward her. "A dollar more an hour for three hundred staff is $624,000 a year. You think the company can wear that kind of cost and not take a hit with the shareholders."

"The shareholders are all called Westerhaven. You're wearing a five thousand dollar watch and a two thousand dollar suit. Let's not even talk about your shoes."

They're Italian leather, handmade, and they were only five hundred dollars. She needs to calm down. We both stop walking when we are toe to toe, her head tipped back and mine forward to keep arguing.

"Only seventy percent of the shareholders are called Westerhaven. The board has a duty to the other thirty percent to get them the best return on their investment we can."

"Was your salary more than $624,000 last year?"

"With your moving bonuses, will yours be more than that this year?"

Layla's cheeks bloom red, and I can't resist. Cupping her jaw with both hands, I lower my head, our lips meeting. Unlike last time, Layla doesn't hesitate, her hands immediately moving to grip my elbows, her mouth opening, and her tongue dancing with mine. Damn straight. One of her hands leaves my elbow, her wrist brushing against my stomach as it heads north, aiming for my tie again. As hot as that was last time, I have other plans involving her fluttering ponytail.

Walking her backward to the couch as I attack her mouth, I reluctantly lift my head when we reach it. Layla's eyes are glazed with passion, her lips swollen. I put both of those looks there. That's a beautiful sight. Grinning down at her, my hands land on her hips, spinning her around until she's facing away from me. My cock twitches at her widening eyes as her face disappears from my sight. My hand lands on the middle of her back, and my other finds her hip as I press her forward.

Layla obligingly bends, her torso heaving under my hand as she leans over, gripping the back of the couch, her ass presented prettily to me. Now, *that's* a beautiful sight. Releasing my eager cock, I tug her pinafore over her hips, exposing her delicate lacy pink panties. Cute. Stripping them down to her knees, I position my cock, rubbing it along her slit, coating it in her eager juices.

"Are you going to screw me, or what?" she gasps. Oh, I'm going to fuck you, sweetheart. That's for sure. Chuckling, I grip both her hips in my hands, slamming forward until she jolts against the couch with a grunt.

"Is that what you wanted?" I growl, withdrawing almost fully and slamming forward again.

"Yes," she moans, the sound snapping something in my brain. I tighten my hold on her hips, hammering into her as hard as I can as she mewls and whimpers, throwing her hips back eagerly to meet my thrusts. That's what I'm talking about.

Before I can get lost in the pleasure of taking what my cock desperately wants, her taunt from Lucas's cocktail party floats through my mind. I'll give her a fucking orgasm to remember. My fingers are more talented than hers. I can guarantee it. Still pounding into her from behind, I release one of her hips, my hand sliding around, my fingers parting her folds as she clenches around my cock. I slick through her juices, finding her clit and circling it with alternating flickers.

"Shit!" she gasps, her hips moving faster, building friction with my fingers.

Layla's orgasm hits unexpectedly, surprising us both with its ferocity. She clings to the couch, slumping a little as her climax finishes. I don't let up, continuing to pound into her, my fingers picking up the pace, strumming her clit like a bass guitar.

"R-Ryan!" she wails, her hips bucking as her pussy flutters, clenching around my cock. Fuck me, that feels amazing. I come with a groan, satisfaction, and pleasure surging through me. How's that for satisfying her? I bet her fingers have never made her shatter twice in ten minutes. Talk about upping my game.

Layla's breath leaves her in a shudder as I withdraw, stepping away and buttoning my fly. Fuck! I need to start carrying a condom on me. She straightens, staring away from me as she fixes her pinafore. Shit. I stare at the back of her head, willing her to turn around. How pissed is she going to be about the whole no-condom thing?

Turning, Layla fixes me with a cold stare, and I fight the urge to wince. Okay. I might be about to get blasted for the whole forgetting the condom. I wait for her to unload on me, but she doesn't.

"Granted, that was better than last time, so maybe a C+."

I blink, my teeth clicking with how fast they snap together. Seriously? A fucking C+? I just rocked her whole damn world. Layla brushes past me, reaching the door and looking over her shoulder to fix me with another glare.

"Besides, it doesn't matter how good you are with your cock. It's not going to make you better at your job."

The door swings shut behind her as I stare, open-mouthed, at it. Did she really say that? Firstly, that was, at the very least, a B+ performance. Secondly, I'm fucking *amazing* at my job, my prowess in the bedroom notwithstanding. Whatever. I'll show her just how great I am at my job in this afternoon's meeting continuation.

HOLD MY HEART

Layla

Taking my seat to Lucas's left, I toy with the iPad laying on the table in front of me. Ryan strides in, stopping to speak with Michael Espinoza at the other end of the table, but I avoid looking in his direction. The board meeting today is to present the quarterly reports and discuss the outcomes of the meeting last week. The one that ended with Ryan and I sniping at each other and screwing over the back of his couch. That was hotter than it should have been.

I lied to him again. I have him a C+ at best... the man gave me two orgasms in one sitting. He's officially a god. I might have also said something mean and untrue about his work abilities. What can I say? We were arguing, and then we were screwing, and I was coming.... My head was all over the place, and I couldn't be held accountable for my mouth going rogue.

I almost completely miss Ryan presenting the quarterly financial position. Too busy trying not to look at him or be turned on. I tune in when Lucas speaks again.

"And the final order of business, staff raises. I believe this was discussed in depth at the heads of department meeting last week?"

Shit. The meeting. I clear my throat, shifting in my seat and fixing my eyes on the table somewhere in the center as Ryan stands again.

"Yes. It was floated at the meeting to raise wages across the board at a rate of one dollar an hour. The consensus is that this would boost staff morale without affecting the bottom line too heavily."

I try to swallow my scoff. I really do try. Unfortunately... everyone at the table hears it, all eyes snapping to me with laser focus. Oops. Grimacing, I clear my throat, toying with my iPad again. I catch Ryan's twitching lips out of the corner of my eye. Ugh, asshole.

"Layla did not agree."

Lucas's eyebrows rise, and there is some murmuring around the table, but no one speaks aloud. Oh well, I've already made my disagreement known, I suppose. Raising my chin, I meet Ryan's electric blue eyes.

"No, I didn't agree. I thought perhaps we could investigate some European studies with promising results discussing employee work/life balance and its positive effects on workplace productivity. I also suggested that maybe two dollars an hour would be a greater performance motivator."

Hold My Heart

"As indeed a ten dollar-an-hour raise would no doubt be," Ryan mocks. My fingers twitch, but I will forever be proud of not flipping him off here and now.

"Oh, I didn't realize going that high was an option. I thought two dollars would be more realistic. You know, for the company's bottom line."

Helen hides a smile behind her water glass, and Greta Hawthorne disguises her chuckle with a hacking cough. Ryan's smile is brittle as he fixes his eyes on me.

"This boardroom is no place for flippancy or sarcasm, Ms. Hall. We are discussing a very serious matter, and if you have nothing of value to add, shall we vote on a blanket dollar-an-hour raise for all employees?"

I grudgingly tap to vote for the measure. I think they should have more, but I will not stop them from having this.

"Unanimous," Lucas decrees, wrapping up the meeting as I glare at the side of Ryan's face, and he studiously ignores my gaze. Lucas shoots me a look as he leaves, but I stay where I am, determined not to stand up until Ryan does. We need to discuss how he spoke to me in front of the entire board. I might have been sarcastic, but I still raised valid points before he drove me to it.

Lucas is the last one out, having paused to speak quietly to Ryan, who smiles and nods, waving him off. As soon as we're alone, the door firmly closed, and the hallway outside the glass walls of the conference room clear, Ryan turns his eyes toward me.

"Care to explain yourself?"

Ouch. You could get frostbite off his tone. I shrug, quirking an eyebrow. "You noted I didn't agree. I stated my case."

"Your tone was unacceptable. This is a professional space. You disrespected the board with your sarcasm."

My mouth drops open. "I didn't disrespect *anyone*. I made my point, you were rude about it, so I got snarky…."

Ryan stands as I trail off, buttoning his suit jacket and raising his eyebrows as he stares down the table at me.

"I expect all members of my board to show respect in this room; to me, to the shareholders, and the other board members."

"Who died and made you emperor?"

Ryan smirks, moving around the table and planting a hand on the polished table to my side, the other on the back of my chair as he leans down, getting all up in my face, our noses only inches apart as I tip my head back, my breath catching as his blows across my cheeks.

"Remember how I said that 70% of the shareholders had the name Westerhaven? Well, 30% of the shareholders have the name Ryan Pierce Westerhaven, so you watch yourself. I will tolerate a certain amount of challenge to my authority if I don't consider it disruptive, but you are skirting that line. You will find yourself out in the cold without a reference if you're not careful and blacklisted from all Westerhaven companies."

I swallow, blinking rapidly, willing myself not to cry as he straightens, fixing his cuffs and looking down at me dismissively.

"You are here as long as you are useful, and your proposals are in the process of being implemented. You don't want to cross me, or you will find you have outlasted your welcome very quickly."

He makes his way fluidly to the door. When he gets there, he pauses, turning to deliver his parting shot.

"And Layla…."

I glance up at the sound of my name, still trying not to cry.

"I don't consider coming all over my cock useful to my company."

My sharp intake of shocked breath is covered by the sounds of Ryan leaving the room and the door closing behind him. Finally alone, the tears flow as I wrap my arms around my middle, sucking in deep breaths. I can't believe he said any of that to me. Respect goes both ways, and he crossed a line. This is our boardroom. Professionalism goes both ways, and the dressing down I received was *not* professional. It was awful. *He* is awful. I can't believe I let him screw me twice.

That won't be happening again. Ever. Not if he was the last man on earth. Not even then.

Chapter Twelve

Ryan

"The employees were incredibly grateful for their pay rises."

I nod to Harold Grantley, one of the more senior managers in the research and development department. Sipping my whiskey, I continue to chat about the recent pay increases that have indeed boosted morale, and hopefully, we will see corresponding performance and productivity growth. My attention is only half on the conversation occurring right now. Across the room, Layla is dressed in a 1950s housewife's attempt at a cocktail dress, complete with a poodle skirt and capped sleeves. She looks ridiculous, and I can't keep my attention off her.

She has been avoiding me since the board meeting last week. I think some of the things I said cut her to the core. I intended to put her in her place, not crush her soul. She's entered the cutthroat corporate world at the highest echelons. She needs to grow thicker skin immediately. If Layla can't handle what I said, she needs to find another profession, because others will say much worse.

This entire evening, Layla hasn't so much as glanced in my direction. She walked right past me when she arrived. The cut direct. I didn't even know that was a thing anymore. I only know it because Mom is obsessed with Jane Austen, and I was an only child. I had to take one for the team because Dad drew the line at Regency movies.

"The new line is almost ready for human trials." Grantley is still talking, though he's not saying anything I haven't read recently in an R&D status report. I nod along, asking the expected questions, though I'm still covertly watching Layla, waiting for my moment. Seriously, it's been hours. This is bordering on sulking, and there's nothing less attractive in a woman than sulking.

Finally, my moment comes. Layla excuses herself, moving along the hallway to the left. Toward the bathrooms.

"If you'll excuse me," I cut Grantley off mid-sentence with an apologetic half-smile, moving across the room in the direction Layla left. I leave my half-empty whiskey tumbler on a server's tray and slip into the hallway after her. Luckily, she's much shorter than I am, so I catch her in half a dozen strides, my fingers closing around her elbow. Layla's head snaps around, her eyes wide, and her mouth opens in outrage. When she sees it's me, irritation flickers across her face. That's better than nothing, which is all I've been getting tonight.

"What do you think you're doing?" she hisses, but I merely lead her into the copy room off the hallway. Kicking the door shut with my foot, I slap on the lights as she whirls to confront me, her skirt doing that spinny thing. Layla's mouth opens again, but I beat her to it.

"What the fuck is your problem?"

She gapes at me for about two seconds, her hands landing on her hips. "*My* problem? I was minding my own business when *you* accosted me. What's your problem?"

Scoffing, I shake my head, crossing my arms over my chest as I survey her. She has to be kidding.

"We aren't twelve. We haven't had a playground disagreement. We're fucking colleagues, and you need to stop acting like a petulant child. Grow the fuck up and grow a backbone."

Layla blinks in shock, her jaw dropping open, mouthing like a fish as her pale skin turns almost bone white. Quick as a flash, her hand snaps out, cracking across my cheek.

Holy fuck. My ear is ringing a little, and my left eye feels like it has exploded. She sure hit the sweet spot there. I don't know if I've ever been slapped before. Punched, sure, I grew up with cousins. But slapped? This is a first. I blink, unsure how to process what just happened. I know she's dressed the part, but did Layla really slap me like some bad parody of a fifties movie?

Layla

Oh my god. Oh my god. Oh my god. What the freaking hell did I do? Oh my god. I assaulted a colleague. Not just *any* colleague. Ryan Pierce *Westerhaven*. The CEO and one of the majority shareholders. I have never done something so impulsively stupid in my entire life. And I let Allison talk me into TPing the Dean's house at UCLA one year.

I'm going to get fired. My breath is cold in my nostrils and loud in my ears. Screw fired. I'm probably going to be charged with assault. Can you go to jail for slapping a billionaire? Probably.

I stare in shock at Ryan. He hasn't moved, eyes wide and filled with the same disbelief flooding me. Shit. My chest is heaving as I try not to panic. I need to leave. But maybe I have to talk to the cops first. I can't tear my eyes away from his face. His dirty blond hair is tousled. His jaw is covered with his usual matching dirty blond stubble.

He looks like he always does… only at this moment, he has a red mark on his left cheek in the shape of my hand. Hell, you can even see my ring mark on the middle finger. I have never slapped anyone, but I must have hit him *hard*.

"O-oh my god. I-I'm so sorry, Ryan...."

I don't get much more of my stumbled apology out when a low growl rumbles out of him. I swallow, taking a step back. His bright blue eyes have darkened, and there isn't enough air in this tiny room. I blink, still too in shock to even flinch, as his hands fly up, grabbing my shoulders roughly and shoving me back against the wall. My breath leaves me in a whoosh as my back connects with the cold metal of a filing cabinet.

"I-I...."

I have no idea what I was going to say – maybe another half-assed apology – when I cut off as Ryan drops to his knees in front of me, his head disappearing under my skirt and petticoats. I... what? What's happening? Oh my *god*!

My panties snap off, and I grip the sides of the filing cabinet, trying to get purchase on the smooth metal as his hands shove my thighs apart. When his lips press against my pussy, I gasp, cutting into a moan as his long fingers part my folds, and his tongue finds my clit, circling it lazily. Oh my god. *Shit*.

This doesn't seem appropriate after I just slapped him, but my body isn't thinking about the consequences right now. It's trying to ride Ryan's face. One of my hands gives up trying to grip a smooth filing cabinet corner, slapping over my mouth as

I whimper. His tongue has abandoned its lazy circles, his hands gripping my ass and hip as he lashes my clit.

When two of Ryan's fingers roughly shove into me, vigorously finger fucking me, I give up on trying to hold it together. My head tips forward, tears gathering in my eyes as I clamp my hand over my mouth so no one hears the animal noises he is drawing out of me and comes to investigate. My hips are straining against his hold, trying to buck against his face as my orgasm crashes against me. I catch my strangled squeal in the palm of my hand, holding my mouth tighter.

My body slumps against the filing cabinet, but immediately, my hips involuntarily buck because Ryan either didn't notice I came, or he doesn't care. Neither his tongue nor his fingers let up for a second. If anything, my orgasm spurs him on. His fingers jab roughly into me again and again, curling and stabbing into my G-spot. Shit. Oh, God. Ohhhhh, *God*. The tears spill over as I squeal into my hand again, coming hard. Again. I didn't even have time to recover from the first time. I didn't think that was even possible.

At least this time, Ryan's fingers slip out of me, his mouth leaving my poor, abused clit. He rises in front of me, his cheek still a little red. I bite my lips, blinking to clear my eyes.

"I…"

"No talking," he growls. My lips snap shut, only to fly open again two seconds later as he sharply tugs me into his arms, lifting me. My legs automatically hook around his waist, my breath whooshing out of me again – well, what breath I had managed to gasp in after my orgasms – as my back hits the wall Ryan shoves me against.

I grip his shoulders, my eyes wide as he fumbles with his fly, his cock springing free, slapping against my core. I bite back a whimper as he guides himself in, his hand moving to grip my ass almost painfully tight. Ryan slams his cock into me, sheathing himself in one rough motion. His mouth captures my gasp at the feeling of him filling me so completely. He kisses me fiercely, my back slapping against the wall in time with his furious thrusts.

If this is my punishment, I think I'm almost being rewarded. It almost doesn't seem fair. My fingers dig into his shoulders as I cling to Ryan for dear life, my ankles locked behind his waist, my pussy gripping his cock with every frenetic movement like it doesn't want to let him go. I almost can't breathe through the constant kisses, but I don't care. It will be worth it if I pass out from lack of oxygen. *This* will be worth it. My third orgasm hits me like a bus. There's no strangled squeal this time. No, I scream against his mouth like a freaking banshee, my legs like jelly noodles, my pussy spasming like an elastic band that has been snapped again and again.

Ryan swallows my screams, still kissing me, his fingers digging into my ass hard enough to leave bruises as he keeps pounding rapidly, driving me into the wall like he intends to leave a Layla-shaped dent. I cling to him, unable to do much more, barely keeping my eyes open in my Zen-like "ultra-orgasmed into a coma" state.

Eventually, Ryan groans against my mouth, his tongue ceasing its plundering as he comes, slumping against me, both of us fitting into that groove we pounded into the wall. After a moment – too soon – Ryan lifts his head, lowering me down the wall. Both our chests are heaving, his eyes glued to mine as he sets me on the ground. My knees wobble, but my legs hold my weight. His hand leaves my ass to tuck his cock away. I swallow, pressing my palm to my heaving chest, unable to look away.

"I'm so sorry for hitting you. That was unacceptable," I mumble, still breathless and unsure if he heard me. Ryan doesn't speak, a hand coming up behind me to tangle in my hair as he tugs my head back, his mouth coming down on mine again to kiss me thoroughly.

This time, when he lifts his head, his cheek is barely red, and I'm having trouble remembering where I am. Oh, that's right. The copy room. Ryan steps back, his fingers leaving my hair as he stoops to collect my torn panties. I reach out for them, but he has already shoved them into his pocket, turning and leaving the room.

I stand in silence, both hands pressed to my chest, trying to get my breathing under control. When I don't look and sound like I've run a marathon, I collect my purse from where I dropped it, fish out my phone, and fix my hair and makeup the best I can. It doesn't need to be perfect. It just needs not to raise any eyebrows while I go directly from this room to my house. I need to get out of this building.

Taking a deep, steadying breath, I flip off the lights, slip out of the room, and quickly make my way downstairs, away from the event, and outside to call a ride share. He doesn't take long to arrive, and I crawl into the backseat, ignoring the driver as I bury my face in my hands.

I can't believe I slapped Ryan. Even if he doesn't press charges, this will be bad for me. I *slapped* him. A co-worker. *At work*. I need to offer my resignation to the board. And I need to do it in person. There is a board meeting tomorrow. I shouldn't be the coward who writes an email. I have to own up to this. Tonight, I need wine. I can't *believe* I slapped him! Who the hell *am* I?

Chapter Thirteen

Ryan

Andy holds out my coffee as I stride into the boardroom. I take it with a nod, turning to Lucas as he approaches me.

"Ms. Hall's solutions are integrating well. The latest financials especially gratified me. The savings from the internal stocktake system alone will cover all pay rises for the year. There won't be any effect on shareholder dividends. I'm sure Bill will be happy to hear that."

I'm sure *Lucas* is happy to hear that. He owns 10% of the company after various share issues as an employee and a very generous retirement package.

"We all knew an RFID system would greatly benefit the bottom line. It's gratifying that it's paid off so quickly."

Lucas shoots me a look. "Maybe it's time to admit that Ms. Hall isn't the enemy."

I flash him a grin, taking a sip of the coffee. "I'm rather enjoying having her as an enemy."

"I have no doubt you are," Lucas smirks. "You've been floundering, waiting to be truly tested again. You were getting complacent."

HOLD MY HEART

I'd be offended, but the man has read me like a book. I haven't had this much fun at the office in years. Before I can speak, Layla walks into the room, distracting me. She's in her black pinafore with a high neckline and ruffles at her wrists. The same outfit she was wearing when I fucked her over the back of the couch in my office. I haven't been able to look at that thing without smirking since then.

She shakes her head when Andy offers her an iced coffee – her go-to drink – and slides into her seat, twisting her fingers in her lap. My eyes narrow as I take my seat, signaling to the rest of the board that the meeting is about to begin. Why does she look nervous? Is it because I chewed her out the last time we were here? She hasn't done anything to irritate me lately, so I can't imagine why she would be worried I'd do it again.

We're not meeting for anything controversial, only to present the latest financials. If anything, she should be smug. Thanks to her solution to Issue One, we're all very happy with the current figures. Lucas clears his throat when everyone is seated, opening the meeting and announcing the quorum and attendees. He taps on his iPad to bring up the first slide on the TV screens behind his head and mine.

"First order of business -"

"May I have the floor?" Layla bursts out, her words louder than she probably intended, her voice shaking a little.

My eyebrows shoot up. They aren't the only ones around the table. Lucas starts a little, turning to her with a smooth smile.

"Of course, Layla. You have the floor."

She offers a shaky smile, taking a deep breath and standing, planting her hands on the table in front of her as though to steady herself. She's tiny, so she doesn't have to bend to make the gesture, as I would have had to.

"It is with great regret that I have to offer the board my resignation. I've enjoyed working here, and I will miss it terribly. It was a fantastic opportunity, and I've learned so much...."

She's still talking, but my ears buzz as I stare at her in shock. What the fuck is this? Did something happen? In her personal life? She seemed fine the other night at the office. More than fine. I remember the look on her face when I took her torn panties with me and left after bringing her to a screaming orgasm.

Lucas is speaking, so I blink hard, focusing on his words. "Is everything all right, Layla? If you need some personal time, the board can approve a leave of absence without accepting your resignation."

Layla offers another wobbling smile, turning to sweep the table, her lips faltering as her eyes pass over me. She draws a deep, quivering breath, shaking her head.

"That's a kind suggestion, but I'm afraid I can't take it, Mr. Keller."

Mr. Keller? When the fuck does she call Lucas, Mr. Keller?

"Th-there was an incident the other night at a business function. I'm afraid -"

Jesus. She's talking about the fucking slap. I surge to my feet, drawing the room's attention to me.

"I think I can shed some light on this matter."

Layla falls silent, her face bone white as she closes her mouth, staring at me, stricken. All eyes are glued to me now; Lucas's promising a world of pain.

"Ms. Hall and I did indeed have a confrontation at the heads of department cocktail event on Friday night. Ms. Hall apologized for her behavior at the time, and I was happy to accept that."

I turn my eyes to her, raising my eyebrows to convey my confusion at this turn of events.

"I had thought our exchange was the end of the matter. As far as I am concerned, the matter *is* closed." My eyes burn into hers. "Ms. Hall, this board does *not* accept your resignation, and I expect this to be the last any of us hear of it."

There is some murmuring around the table as eyes turn stay on Layla, who is still bone white. Lucas nods stiffly to me, turning his face back to Layla as well.

"Ms. Hall?"

She jumps, sinking into her seat, her fingers fidgeting on the desk. "I'd like to thank Mr. Pierce Westerhaven for his understanding. I withdraw my resignation."

Lucas nods as I slowly retake my seat. Greta Hawthorne, seated beside Layla, reaches over and squeezes her forearm, still lying on the table. When Layla glances at her, Greta offers her a kind smile and a nod, moving her attention back to Lucas, who quickly runs through the orders of business, ending the meeting as soon as possible.

Layla is the first out of the room, Helen Lawlor patting me on the shoulder as she hurries after her. Everyone else trickles out, looking awkward, either offering half smiles or avoiding looking at me altogether. Eventually, only Lucas and I remain, the door swinging closed behind Andy. Lucas fixes his eyes on me, his fingers steepled in front of his mouth, his elbows planted on the arms of his chair.

"A confrontation?"

I fight the urge to wince at the accusation in his words. I sigh, sitting back in my chair, gamely meeting Lucas' eyes. "We exchanged words."

"And yet, only she apologized."

"Only she slapped me."

Lucas' eyebrows shoot up, but he chuckles, shaking his head. "She was going to resign because she slapped you?"

HOLD MY HEART

"I am a co-worker, I suppose. It seems overkill. We're not exactly sitting in cubicles in front of a computer."

Lucas sighs, dropping his hand to stroke his palm over the smooth wooden tabletop. "She slapped you. You're happy to let that go?"

I bite back a smile at the memory of fucking Layla into the wall after she slapped me. As far as I'm concerned, it was foreplay, not assault.

"I can assure you that I harbor no hard feelings toward Ms. Hall about the incident. As I said, as far as I'm concerned, that's in the past. I'm happy to go to her office and assure her of that."

"I think that would be best."

Grimacing, I nod to Lucas, shoving out of my seat and leaving the room. The man is retired, and he's still bossing me around. Typical. Moving along the floor toward Layla's office, I step inside, my eyes finding the frizzy-haired little mouse Layla hired as her secretary. She shoves to her feet as I walk into the outer office space.

"M-Mr. Pierce Westerhaven."

"I'm here to see Ms. Hall. Is she in?"

She nods, hurrying around her desk. She stumbles to a halt as I raise my hand.

"I'll go through. Why don't you take an early lunch."

Her wide eyes dart between the door and me. She nods uncertainly, collecting her things and edging out of the room, keeping her eyes on me like I'm a wild animal. When the outer door swings shut behind her, I continue to Layla's office, rapping my knuckles on the door.

"Come in, Karly."

I open the door, sticking my head around it. "And if I'm not Karly, can I still come in?"

She jumps, shoving to her feet, her cheeks flaming. "R-Ryan. Y-yes. Sorry. I wasn't expecting you."

Stepping inside, I close the door behind me, offering a smile. "I sent Karly for an early lunch."

"Oh. Okay." Layla stands still, her fingers brushing over her desk as she watches me. She's still nervous. I'm not used to it. Lucas was right. We need to clear the air. But first, we need to talk about what the fuck she was thinking, trying to resign over something so stupid.

Layla

Ryan glares at me, shoving his hands into his suit pockets, his hair tousled. I bite my lip, waiting for whatever is coming. I deserve it.

"What the fuck were you thinking, resigning?"

I cringe at the venom in his tone. Is he... angry that I tried to offer my resignation? What did he think would happen? I *slapped* him. Does he not remember that part? The sex was great, but the slap is seared into my brain. The noise it made, the mark it left, the look of shock on his face.

"I thought you would be happy that I'm gone."

Ryan makes a choking noise, still glaring at me. "What makes you think that?"

Uh, every interaction we've ever had? Does he not remember telling me that coming all over his cock isn't considered a useful skill for the company?

"You... I... we... we clash. A lot."

Waving his hand dismissively, Ryan scoffs at the idea, like it means nothing to him. Surely, he can't enjoy coming to work and being confrontational with me daily. Isn't that draining for him?

"We might clash, but our little competition improves the company. Weren't you paying attention to the figures Lucas presented today?"

Yeah, they were good. The RFID savings offset the pay rises. The shareholders will be happy. Ryan must be satisfied with that. But I can't just forget that I assaulted a colleague. How is everyone brushing over that part? How is Ryan? I wrap my arms around my waist, lifting my eyes to his chin. I'm too much of a coward to raise them further.

"I don't know if I can work with someone I physically assaulted," I whisper. There is total silence, and I risk a peek at his face, blinking in surprise at the smirk fixed there as he studies me. He removes his hands from his pockets, spreading them in front of him in the universal gesture for "what about this?"

"What if I hit you back? Could you get over it then? An eye for an eye?"

Wh-what? Does he want to slap me? In the face? He can't be serious. My mouth drops open, and I blink hard.

"I don't... understand."

Ryan gestures at my desk. "Come around here, bend over the desk and put two hands on it."

How does that equate to him slapping me in the face? This is so confusing. Despite my brain stuttering, trying to figure out what is happening, my feet are moving, carrying me around the desk until I'm facing it, my back to Ryan. I let out a shaky breath, bending forward to plant my hands on the desk. I'm glad he can't see my face. My cheeks are flaming as I remember the last time I was in a similar position, over the back of his office couch. I don't think that's what is happening here.

Ryan's footsteps are soft as he approaches, and his hand caresses my back, my skirt flipping up over it. My cheeks are redder than Mercury right now. This is the same outfit I wore when we screwed over the back of his couch, and he flipped up the skirt the same. I suck in a breath as he tugs my panties down. I thought I was getting slapped... but maybe he wants to have sex first?

I'm about to ask what is happening when I jolt forward, a squeal slipping out of me as his palm cracks against my bare ass. Ouch. I wince, sucking a breath between my teeth as Ryan's voice surrounds me.

"Are we even?"

Are we? Emotions I can't quite pinpoint swirl inside me, and I bite back a gasp at the feeling of wetness between my thighs. I think his spanking just turned me on. I should agree, and we can move on. But my mouth goes rogue.

"I-I don't know."

His soft inhale has my pussy muscles clenching. I jolt forward again as his palm cracks against my other ass cheek. Shit. That stings. He doesn't speak and doesn't hit me again, his hand moving between my legs. My cheeks flame at the thought that he will know how wet this spanking just made me. But he doesn't mention it, shoving two fingers inside me, pumping them slowly.

"What about now?"

A moan slips from my lips, my hips moving of their own accord, pushing back against his slow fingers. "Yeah. Maybe we are even."

"I thought that might be the case. Now, stay like that."

I'm happy to oblige as Ryan's fingers pick up the pace, fucking me as his other hand lands on my lower back, his fingers caressing my bare flesh as he drives me insane with his thrusting fingers. Panting, I stare at the polished wooden desk in front of my face, my fingers splaying as I brace myself. Oh god, I'm so close. A whimper breaks free of my lips as I push my hips back faster, spurring Ryan's fingers on.

"Come for me. That's a good girl."

Shit. He can't say stuff like that! My inner muscles spasm around his fingers, trying to hold them inside me as I come, my breath shuddering out of me. Ryan's fingers change from stabbing into me to stroking my insides. It's a weird feeling that has me squirming. But before I can react, they slip out of me, and he tugs me upright, his hand closing around my ponytail as he pulls my head back, his mouth covering mine in a punishing kiss.

"No more talk of resigning. Or 'the slap'," Ryan murmurs against my lips. I nod, staring as he smirks, turning and striding out of the room, tugging the door closed behind him. I blink after him, scrambling to tug my panties up from around my knees. What was that? I'm shocked that he wants me to stick around after all our run-ins. I don't know how to explain it, but it feels like things between us have changed. Like… we're kind of on the same side. Ugh, it's probably just the orgasm aftershocks talking… isn't it?

Chapter Fourteen

Ryan

Flipping off the TV, I shove off the sectional couch, drop the remote on the coffee table and move to the panel off the open-plan kitchen. It's three in the afternoon on a Sunday, and I'm not expecting any deliveries or guests. Hitting the button, the panel screen lights up with the security shot of the front door. My lips tug into a grin. Why is Layla standing at my front door, cradling a basket? She looks like Little Red Riding Hood, except her 1950s poodle skirt dress isn't red; it's lime green. How the fuck does the woman look sexy in it?

Jogging down two flights of stairs, I walk through the long foyer, opening the door and grinning as I lean against the doorframe. "What brings you here? There's no board event this weekend."

Layla flushes, holding up the basket, which I can now see is packed to the brim with fruit.

"You're delivering fruit?"

She rolls her eyes, handing the basket over. I take it, bemused and still unsure why she's giving it to me.

"Think of it as a peace offering."

HOLD MY HEART

My eyebrows shoot up. "Why am I getting a peace offering?"

"Hey, I went to a farmer's market and picked every piece there. This is a nice gesture."

"And what's brought this nice gesture on?"

Layla shrugs, wrapping her arms around her waist. "We have a truce, right?"

My lips twitch. I suppose you could call it that. We haven't clashed since her spanking last Monday. A truce... that's one way to describe it.

"Soooo, can I come in?"

Right. Because we're still standing in the entryway. "Sure."

Stepping back, I let her in, closing the frosted glass door behind her. I grip the basket handle, gesturing for her to lead the way to the stairs.

"I'll give you the tour."

Layla nods as we walk along the hallway and up to the first floor. I gesture dismissively to the right.

"Bathroom, laundry." We peek around the corner to the left. "Games room, my bedroom, and a guest bathroom are around to the left again."

"Uh-huh." Layla nods, murmuring her agreement, her eyes glued to the view past the pool table and wet bar. I don't blame her. It's a marvelous view of LA. It gets better as you get higher.

"Come on up."

"Oh." Layla starts as my hand lands on her lower back, guiding her up the next set of stairs to the second level. I jab my thumb to the right.

"Another guest bedroom, and a bathroom, if you need it."

Layla nods again, her eyes once again glued to the view, this time over the top of my living room furniture, including my two large sectional couches.

"Wow," she whispers reverentially. Grinning, I set the fruit basket on the large, black marble-topped kitchen island, propping myself up by my elbow as I watch her mouth drop open, and she slowly turns to take in the full, 180-degree view.

"You have a lovely home," she murmurs, her mouth still hanging open. She hasn't spared much of a glance at the house. I think she means I have a lovely view. No arguments there. I can't help a dig. After all, it's kind of our thing. Still propped against the kitchen island, I grin at the side of her awestruck face.

"You know, if you don't close your mouth, I'll shove my cock in it."

A gorgeous shade of red blooms across her pale cheeks as her mouth snaps shut, her head whipping around so her huge, wide eyes can land on me. She doesn't speak, and my lips twitch into a smirk as I study her. Finally, I take pity, nodding to her.

"So, apart from the peace offering fruit basket. You're just here to snoop around my house?"

Layla continues to flush, shrugging and hugging her waist again. "Actually, I had an idea that I wanted to run by you. You know, to see if you had any input before I take it to the board."

Uh, what? My eyebrows shoot up, and I straighten from the kitchen island, studying her more closely.

"You want my input on something before you take it to the board?"

Layla squirms, shrugging defensively. "Well… yeah. You always have ideas and make changes that the board seems to like anyway, so I thought… why not save everyone some time and take the joint proposal to them."

I can see the wisdom in her words. Her idea to come to me and spitball a joint proposal makes me feel things. Things I can't explain. Closing the distance between us, I slide my fingers into her thick, heavy hair, tilting her head back to search her light, fiery eyes. Layla's lips part as my head lowers, my mouth covering hers and my tongue dancing along the seam of her lips.

She parts them with a sigh, her tongue fencing with my own as my hands slide down her back, cupping her ass and lifting her against me. Layla's arms snake around my neck as her legs wrap around my waist. Perfect. Now I have to get her downstairs.

The guest bedroom on this level is made up – I never know when someone will drop in – but I want Layla in my bed. The stairs are out because I'm not ready to stop tasting her delicious, plump pink lips, so I carry her to the elevator, jabbing the down button. Layla breaks the kiss, looking around in surprise as I step inside.

"You have a home elevator?"

"Yes." I grab her head, bringing our lips together again. Less talking, more kissing. Layla moans against my mouth, adequately distracted as the elevator takes us down a level. She doesn't look back up as I navigate through the games room and into the main bedroom.

Tipping Layla onto the bed, I quickly strip to my trunks, trying to decide which part of this intriguing outfit I will open first. I settle for her strappy heels, stripping them off and dropping them onto the floor beside my jeans and polo shirt. Layla giggles, her eyes locked on my chest – a bit of an ego boost that I'm managing to keep her attention off the glorious view of the city spread out before us through the floor-to-ceiling feature windows behind me – and I slowly strip her poodle skirt and top off, leaving her stretched out on my gunmetal gray Egyptian cotton sheets in her forest green lacy panties and bra.

I don't know if she had an inkling we might end up in bed and dressed up for me or if she's always wearing lingerie under her prissy little outfits, but I like the idea of the latter, especially if I'm the only one who has any idea of their existence. Right now, they'd look good on my plush gray rug. I strip them off, my fingers skimming over Layla's soft flesh. Shucking my trunks, I come down on top of her, my mouth finding every bit of available skin it can.

Layla writhes and moans, bucking her hips and pressing her wet core against my stomach.

"Ry-*an*," she whines, twining her legs around mine. Grinning against her breast, I bite down on her nipple, laving it with my tongue to take away the sting as Layla's breath hisses between her teeth, and she sighs. Positioning my cock at her dripping entrance, I take my weight on my forearms, lifting to hold her gaze as I sink into her.

"So fucking good," I murmur, lowering my head to tease the side of her throat with my lips and tongue. Layla's arms and legs tighten around me as her pussy muscles grip my cock.

"*You* feel good," she whispers, her eyes fluttering closed, her voice breathy. My smug smirk presses against the fragrant skin of her neck. That's a change of tune from all her C+s, and a welcome one. I could set a punishing pace, but I'm enjoying this slow, sensual one. Nipping Layla's earlobe, I press my nose against the side of her face, taking her jasmine scent deep into my lungs as my cock bottoms out in her pussy, slowly withdrawing and pressing firmly back in.

Layla's hips are rising and falling with my slow, deliberate thrusts. She doesn't seem in any hurry to speed things up, but that doesn't mean I can't wring a few orgasms out of her. My hand creeps down, my fingers parting her folds and finding her clit, circling it as leisurely as my thrusts.

"So good, Ryan," she whimpers, her mouth falling open and her eyes squeezing more firmly closed. Yeah, she is. I change to flicking her clit, my thrusts speeding up until I hammer into her.

"Yes!" she screams, her eyes flying open as her pussy spasms, milking my cock. As much as I would like to draw this out, I'm okay coming with her and fucking her again later.

Groaning, I hold deep, releasing inside her and nibbling against her neck as she settles floppily into the comfortable bed. I don't want to crush her, so I roll us over until she's cradled on my chest.

Layla's eyes find the view, and she sighs contentedly. "I'm glad you didn't let me see that on the way in. I totally would have gotten distracted."

Smirking, I drop a kiss on her temple, turning my eyes to the view and savoring it. There's nothing better than looking at the city stretching below me after I've fucked myself into contentment.

Layla

My eyes drink in the glorious, uninterrupted sight of LA before us. This is a view anyone could get used to. I don't live near West Hollywood, where we are now, but if I ever had the money, I'd move into this neighborhood.

A contented sigh slips from my lips as Ryan's fingers stroke through my hair. I sneak a peek, but he's still looking at the view, almost absentmindedly stroking. It still feels nice, even if he's unaware he's doing it. Ryan's eyes flicker toward me, the corners of his lips tugging upward. Oops, caught looking. He doesn't stop stroking my hair, but he does keep looking at me, so I turn my head a little to meet his gaze.

"Let's hear your idea."

My cheeks are beginning to burn again. Normally, I would send through a fully fleshed-out proposal and field questions. This is different. It's like I'm baring my soul to him without the neatly typed and spell-checked proposal between us.

"It has to do with inventory management."

"I'm all ears."

I would roll my eyes – how ridiculous does that sound? A billionaire playboy is all ears about *inventory management*. Except he does look interested. I still have to pinch myself that he enjoys this stuff. Or, at the very least, he *cares*.

"Now that the RFID tracking is running and working well, I thought about tackling the rest of the spoilage issue."

Ryan studies me for a moment, and I brace for him to scoff and shut me down.

"The wastage caused by not tracking expiration dates?" he guesses. I blink. That's not shutting me down.

"Yeah. That."

Ryan nods, his fingers still stroking – I'll take that as a good sign. "What's your solution?"

I open my mouth to respond, but it turns into a sigh of pleasure as Ryan's fingers stroke down my hair and over the naked flesh of my back. Ugh, he's distracting me. He knows what he's doing, too – I can see the flash of amusement in his eyes. I'll show him!

Hold My Heart

Clearing my throat, I fix him with a steely glare. Ryan meets it gamely, still caressing my lower back. Okay, I can do this while he's making me squirm. I'm a professional.

"I think we could have a program written that utilizes the RFID data. Then it could bring up a system alert when an expiration date for a batch is approaching. It would streamline everything. We could even set up a corresponding alert that it's time to reorder stock."

A frown draws Ryan's eyebrows down, though his fingers still skate over my skin. Okay, that's a *super* simplified version of the idea, but I also have a rough proposal drafted on my phone that I can email him. I'm about to suggest that when the frown disappears, and he groans, his mouth covering mine as he tugs me against his chest, rolling onto his back.

I kiss him back eagerly, my legs hugging his waist. Ryan's hands grip my ass, lifting me as his cock prods against my entrance. Oh, yes. My proposal can wait for *this*.

Dropping a kiss on my shoulder, Ryan climbs out of bed, disappearing into the gray brushed marble ensuite bathroom off the bedroom. I smile to myself, my eyes finding the glorious view again. I can't believe someone I know actually lives like this.

"Still enjoying the view?"

My eyes snap to the bathroom door, where Ryan is lounging, his shoulder against the doorframe. He must have a closet in there because he's dressed in a Duke sweatshirt and loose linen trousers, not the jeans and polo on the floor at the base of the bed with my pile of clothes.

"How do you even leave the house?"

Ryan chuckles, shoving away from the door and moving into the room to pick up my clothes and carefully lay them on the bed. His eyes roam over me, and I resist the urge to tug the coverlet up. He can look at my naked breasts! He had his mouth all over them ten minutes ago.

"I'd never get any work done if I had you here distracting me, looking like that."

My cheeks flame. That was... kind of the nicest thing he's ever said to me. I guess my peace offering fruit basket worked. The bed dips as Ryan places a hand on it, leaning down to brush a kiss over my lips.

"I'll leave you to use the bathroom and freshen up. Meet me on the roof. The stairs are near the guest bathroom upstairs. We'll run through your idea."

"Okay."

That was breathier than I intended. Oops. Ryan's pupils dilate, and his nostrils flare... but he has more self-control than me and straightens, grinning as he leaves the room.

Hold My Heart

The door swings shut behind him, and I savor one last look at the view before moving into the bathroom. The glimpse of gray brushed marble I caught is the theme of the whole room. I didn't know a bathroom could scream "rich," but this one does.

My eyes linger on the waterfall showerhead. Oh my god. Are those... wall jets? My teeth sink into my lower lip as I peek back through the bedroom, my eyes lingering on the firmly closed door. I mean... he did say to freshen up. That means a shower. Right? Whatever. I'm doing it. This might be my only chance. Two towels are hanging on the fancy heated towel rack, so it won't be weird. Flicking on the mixer, I watch with wide eyes as water cascades from *everywhere*. Yeah. I need to be inside this thing. Now.

Giggling, I step in, my laughter cutting into a moan as all the jets hit me. This is heavenly. Screw the view. How does he leave the *shower*?

Right. He's waiting for me upstairs. For work. I shower faster than I would like to, reluctantly shutting the water off and sighing as the jets cease. That was lovely.

I step out of the shower, snagging the towel furthest away. I'm assuming Ryan would use the closer one. I would. I'm not sure what to do with the towel, I don't see a laundry hamper, so I carefully rehang it, searching for my clothes. While I'm here, I remake his bed. My eyes linger on the view again. No. He really is waiting for me. I can't get distracted. More.

Leaving the bedroom, I go back to the stairs, climbing to the top level. He said the roof, though. I'm looking straight at the bottom of another set of stairs. That must be up to the roof. I head up, emerging from the stairwell into a white-walled study with abstract art and neatly stacked bookshelves. One wall is completely glass, and I actually whimper. Seriously. This is his *house*? The glass door in the glass wall is open, and I step out, my eyes sweeping over the Garden of Eden he's got going on up here.

The grass is fake, but it's soft and springy. There's a wraparound wet bar with at least eight barstools and trees in planter boxes offering shade over two plush wicker couches to the side. There's an infinity pool that is an insane shade of blue and has a freaking *waterfall* at one end.

The pool stretches away from this bar area, and if you swim across, you get to another rooftop balcony area with a fire pit, wooden bench seating around it, and sun loungers. The view is… insane. Of all the insane things up here, the view is the most incredible.

Ryan grins as he waves to me from the bar. He has a cheese platter and is pouring two glasses of white wine. I cross to him, sinking onto a bar stool and dragging my eyes away from the view to smile at him.

HOLD MY HEART

"You have a lovely home."

I think I already said that, but Ryan doesn't correct me, laughing instead as he sits beside me, tapping his glass against mine.

"The proposal."

"Right. Sorry. The view distracted me."

He laughs again as I dig my phone out of my purse, tapping into my emails to send him the rough draft.

"I've sent you a more in-depth description."

"Hang on."

Ryan disappears into the study, grabbing an iPad out of the desk and returns. He taps around, and I sample the cheese and sip my wine. My fingers linger on the small bunch of grapes on the fancy wooden board. I wonder if these are some of the grapes I brought in my basket.

I'm torn between admiring the view and studying Ryan's face as he reads over my rough draft. I want to analyze every micro-expression. But that's probably not healthy, so I turn my eyes to the stunning view. The sun is starting to set, and I never want to leave. Maybe I should be nice to him until we're friends. Then I can be his roommate.

"This could work."

I almost jump as Ryan's voice cuts through my reverie. My eyes snap back to him, my cheeks flaming. Ryan is watching me with amusement as he nibbles on a piece of blue cheese smeared over a very expensive cracker.

"Y-you think so?"

Ryan nods slowly, spinning the iPad so I can see some of the notes he has added. He sips his wine as I drag the iPad closer, hunching over it to read them. He hasn't torn my proposal to shreds – so that's nice. Scanning through the comments, I bite back a smile. I was right to come here and ask him for his input. All his ideas make the proposal better.

"May I?" I murmur, tapping my fingernail against the iPad screen.

"By all means."

Nodding, I start typing up the proposal properly, only stopping to ask Ryan for clarification on a comment here and his input on the wording there. By the time I finish, the sun has sunk low over the city, and the bottle of wine is empty. Ryan looks up from where he is reading over the completed proposal with a grin, plucking up his wine glass. He taps it against mine and drains the last mouthful as I copy the gesture.

"I think this was a productive venture."

I blush, toying with the stem of my wine glass as Ryan pulls up a town car app on his phone. I guess the interlude is over.

"We'll present it to the board at the meeting later this week. I think they'll like it."

"I hope so. It's an area that needs improvement, and this is a good way to do it."

"Very good." Ryan flashes me a smile, standing as he does. I quickly slide off the barstool, nowhere near as elegantly as he managed – damn being short – and walk inside as he gestures.

We make our way down the three flights of stairs to the front door, and Ryan peers outside. "Your town car is here."

"Th-thanks."

Another smile tugs at his lips as he cups my jaw, lowering his head. Oh, so I'm not exactly being kicked out. I cling to his sweatshirt with both hands as his tongue traces the line of my lips, slipping inside when I part them. I fence back with my own tongue, savoring this kiss. I don't know if this truce is just for the afternoon or until our joint proposal is presented… or if it's a longer-term thing, but I'm going to enjoy it while it lasts. Especially if it includes kisses like *this*.

Ryan's hands drop away from my cheeks as he lifts his head. Boo. I wasn't nearly done kissing him yet. He smirks, his thumb brushing over my cheek, and as I turn, he taps my ass. My breath catches, and I throw what I hope is a flirty smile over my shoulder as I hurry to the car.

The driver holds open the door, and I slide in. As it closes, I peek through the window, but Ryan has already disappeared inside, the imposing front door already closed. Well, I wasn't expecting him to stand and wave. Was I?

Chapter Fifteen

Ryan

I accept the coffee from Andy, nodding along to Hartley Kemp's conversation, but my eyes keep flickering to the door, waiting for Layla to walk through it. I have never presented a joint proposal to the board before. The document was sent around earlier in the week for everyone's perusal, so today will mainly be answering questions and the all-important vote to implement.

Lucas moves to his seat at the foot of the table as Layla walks in with Helen Lawlor, smiling and accepting the iced coffee Andy holds out and catching my eye. She offers me a small smile, taking her seat as Lucas gestures toward the table.

Nodding to Hartley, I slide into my chair, setting down my coffee and plucking up the iPad to follow along with the meeting schedule as Lucas runs through the housekeeping matters.

"First order of business, the proposal sent through by Ryan."

Standing, I leave the iPad on the table, extending my hand, palm up toward Layla. "This is a joint proposal with Ms. Hall if she wants to join me."

Pink tinges at Layla's cheeks and a few amused looks are exchanged around the room as she shoves to her feet, scurrying around the table to stand beside me. It's her proposal, so I hand over the clicker with a nod.

"Oh, th-thanks, Mr. Pierce Westerhaven." She takes it, turning with wide eyes to the room, clearing her throat to run through the presentation we put the finishing touches on this morning.

There are surprisingly few questions, and Lucas beams, tapping his iPad. "Thank you, Ryan and Layla. I think everyone is ready to put it to a vote if you could take your seats."

Layla flashes me another smile as she hurries back to her seat, snatching up her iPad. I bite back an amused smirk, taking my place and casting my vote in favor of our proposal.

"Unanimous," Lucas' voice booms out. My eyes immediately find Layla's down the table, and her smile now is anything but tentative. Damn, we're a good team when we work together. I didn't mind the extra-curriculars we indulged in while running through her proposal, either.

"It's nice to see you two finally working together."

My thoroughly pleasant reminiscences are interrupted by Michael Espinoza's amused comment. Layla's cheeks turn cherry red, and at least two other board members hide laughter behind hurried coughs.

"Let's just say Ms. Hall and I have discovered we work better together than pitted against each other."

My remark is met by general laughter and a bemused look from Lucas. "Might I remind you that you were the only ones pitting you against each other."

"It was fun," I protest, to more laughter. My eyes turn in Layla's direction again. She's looking marginally less mortified now. Did she really think they hadn't noticed our animosity? It was pretty fucking obvious. They don't sit on this board because of their net worth, but because of their brains. They weren't going to miss that.

Ha. I bet she thinks it was unprofessional to have a workplace rivalry that people noticed. She might be a good COO, but she's also adorably naïve. I guess her dress sense suits her more than I realized.

Layla

Humming along to the pop rock spilling from my speakers, I tap my toes to the tune, flicking through Pinterest ideas for cute back decks on my phone.

I want to spruce up the back area. The gardening company has done wonders with the landscaping and keeping everything looking glorious. My boring deck with nothing but a wrought iron table and two matching chairs is letting the side down.

The phone buzzes, and the notification bar drops down as my mouth falls open.

RYAN: Come over. Need to run through some stuff for work. Department issues. I'll send a town car.

The phone buzzes again, and an inhuman squeak presses out of me at the notification that the town car is on its way. I'm in *sweats*! I haven't brushed my hair today. With a shriek, I leap off the couch, sprinting upstairs, stripping off my clothes as I go. My phone bounces across the bed as I launch it, wrenching open my closest and scouring my clothes.

My eyes land on my lilac, long-sleeved ruffle dress. It's cute and will work with an updo, which is necessary. I don't have time to take on my hair today. Tossing the dress onto my bed with my phone, I dash into the shower, clipping my hair out of the way. No time to wash it – it would still be dripping wet when I arrived at his house!

HOLD MY HEART

I shave my legs in record time, toweling myself down and hurrying to pin my hair up. I settle on an easy twist, pinning the whispers from around my face and quickly applying a lick of makeup. That will have to do. My phone beeps. Shit. That's the town car arriving. Wriggling into my dress, I zip it up, snagging my heeled Mary Janes and clipping them on. Done. Perfect timing. Dropping my phone into my purse, I hurry down the stairs, throwing the door open and waving to the driver as he slides out of the car, holding open the back door for me.

Why am I nervous? A colleague has asked me to his house on the weekend to run through some department issues. That's nothing to be anxious about. Except... the last time I was at his home, we had sex. Twice. And it was glorious. And that last kiss.... No! I can't get ahead of myself. Digging out my phone, I obsessively check my makeup. I had to do it so quickly. I need to make sure it is on point. Just in case.

"We've arrived, Ms. Hall."

Right. I snap my phone off, shoving it into my purse. Did the driver have a smirk on his face just then? I think he had a smirk on his face. Ugh. He was probably laughing at how stupid I looked, checking my makeup with my phone. Kill me now.

The door opens, and I suck in a deep breath, gathering my purse and sliding out. It's never elegant. I'm too short to get out of a car gracefully. There's no firmly placing a foot. It's all slide, and hope for the best. Thankfully, Ryan isn't exactly standing at the door, watching me. That would be humiliating. The driver moves back to the car as I set my shoulders, marching to the front door and ringing the fancy doorbell.

There's no buzzing like an apartment this time. Instead, within minutes, the door swings open, and Ryan grins down at me. My breath catches. He's dressed in jeans again, but this time, he's just in a T-shirt. Sure, it's a Duke T-shirt, but it's still a T-shirt. Somehow, he looks even more informal than in his sweatshirt and lounge pants. He looks... really sexy. I'm used to seeing Ryan in a suit – which he kills – but this is more... intimate.

"Come on in."

I shiver as I step inside, feeling every inch of the sweep his eyes do over my outfit. Hey, this is the best I could do on short notice, and it's cute!

"To the roof?"

"Living room," he calls from behind as he follows me up the stairs. Am I swinging my hips in a sexy manner, or is it too contrived and obvious? Ugh. Get it together, Layla! Stop overthinking things. He probably isn't even *looking* at your ass.

I risk a peek as we round the top of the stairs to the next flight. Eek! He's staring at my ass. Deep breaths. My eyes snap forward, and I keep walking. Don't think about it. Don't try to walk differently. Just. Be. Normal!

I reach the living room, and my eyes land on the view, my freak out about Ryan's eyes on me forgotten as a contented sigh whispers out of me. I've missed that view.

"As good as you remember?"

He's teasing me, but that's okay. This view is worth it.

"Yeah," I breathe. I'm answered with a chuckle, another shiver working its way up my spine as Ryan's hand lands on my lower back, caressing softly as he guides me toward the sleek lines of the white fabric sectional. I sink into it, tearing my eyes away from the view to the cheese platter and white wine laid out on the coffee table. The man knows how to host, that's for sure.

"No grapes?"

Ryan chuckles, taking a seat next to me and pouring two glasses of wine.

"No one brought me any from the farmer's markets."

I press my lips together to keep from smiling as I accept my glass. I *knew* those grapes on the last platter were from my basket. That's kind of super sweet.

Ryan gestures to the iPad lying on the table, and I sip my wine as I pick it up, flicking through the report. I read this yesterday in the office. The R&D department is having issues.

Their new junior manager is struggling with the increased responsibilities, affecting productivity.

"They seem to be handling the job well," I hedge. Ryan snickers, popping an olive into his mouth and waggling his eyes as I swallow, watching his lips. He should do that again. I liked watching that.

"Focus, Ms. Hall, and I'll put these lips all over you when we're done."

I should be professional, but I can't. Now he's mentioned it, I can't think of anything but his lips on me, and I have to pout. Ryan's eyes dip to my lips, and a low growl rumbles out of him. So. Hot. I shouldn't egg him on, but my tongue has a mind of its own, darting out and sweeping across my parched lower lip. Ryan's eyes follow it hungrily.

"Or now. Now works too," he mutters, taking both our glasses and placing them on the coffee table before crowding me, forcing me backward until I'm lying sideways on the couch.

I reach for him, but Ryan isn't looking at my face. He has sunk to his knees beside the couch, carefully lifting and folding my skirt until it's neatly piled on my stomach.

"I knew it," he murmurs – whatever that means – but I'm not pondering his words much longer as Ryan leans over, his lips and *tongue* teasing me through my lacy purple panties. Ugh. *Yes*.

HOLD MY HEART

Keeping the lace covering my pussy, Ryan spreads me wide with his thumbs, sucking on my clit. Oh my! His tongue occasionally massages, pressing the scratchy lace where I am most sensitive before sucking again. This is *heaven*. With a moan, I reach down, sliding my fingers through his messy, dirty blond hair. He can do this whenever he feels the urge. I never really thought about lingerie being *part* of the sexual act before... but I'm never going to be able to think of it separately again.

I mean, I always wear it. I'm short, and I have a ... particular dress sense. Wearing lingerie makes me feel sexy. I wear it for myself, but lately, I'm getting a kick out of how Ryan looks at me when he sees it. It's crazy empowering.

Ryan sucks harder, his tongue swirling, making sure every single bit of my clit is massaged with scratchy lace. The building pressure low in my stomach spills over, and I buck my hips as I come with a sigh.

Lifting his head, Ryan grins smugly, carefully covering me with my dress again. "Now, can we focus on the department issues?"

He's a cocky bastard, but he has every right to be. I'm still shaking from the aftershocks of the orgasm those smirking lips just delivered.

"Sure. What did you want to discuss?" My voice is super breathy, but I just came all over his face, so I'm not to blame.

Ryan's pupils dilate at the sound, but he simply clears his throat, retaking his seat and adjusting himself as he reaches for his wine.

There is a sizeable bulge in his jeans. I should probably offer to take care of that for him – he did take care of me – but he gestures to the iPad before I can make the offer. Aw. He's being a gentleman. I have no idea why, maybe because he's a cocky, rich, prickly ass, but the idea of him denying himself is making my stomach flutter. Weird.

"I want to discuss the fact that the staff has been complaining that since Aaron Livingstone was made junior manager, his attitude to his fellow staff has been… unpleasant."

My eyes dart back to the second tab Ryan has open. An email from the department head. Ah. Bullying complaints. Yeah, some people can't handle the ego boost that comes with a promotion into a managerial position. You give them an inch of power over their fellow workers, and they'll snatch as many miles as possible.

"I had fellow managers like that when I was a junior manager with Haven Freight," I admit. Ryan nods, sipping his wine as he studies me.

"Then you are the right person to discuss this with."

HOLD MY HEART

"You need to have a plan in place. If you let it go, you'll lose good staff. People aren't going to want to continue working under someone like this."

"So, we fire them?"

Shit. No mercy. I roll my eyes, and Ryan grins at me.

"I'm guessing that's a no?"

"He needs a written warning. But you need to have an escalation plan in place. It's best to lay it out in the written warning, so he knows what is coming down the line at him if he doesn't change his behavior."

"What do you suggest?"

Wrinkling my nose, I focus on the view, sipping my wine as I mull it over. I hate stuff like this. Discussing a plan toward termination is never fun because that's a *person* on the other side of that plan, with a life, bills, and stuff like that.

"He needs to make a general apology to the staff and attempt to change his behavior. Have a probationary period where it can be reviewed. Stuff like that. The next step would be moving him back down to general staff and replacing him as a junior manager. Termination would be the last resort."

"That's a lot of chances for a bully."

"I gave you lots of chances. You came around in the end."

Ryan's eyebrows shoot up as he chuckles, his hand moving to toy with the skirt of my dress. It's a surprisingly intimate gesture, and I manage to hide my breath catching by taking another sip of wine.

"I gave you lots of chances, too," he protests. I don't manage to hide my eye roll.

"You were trying to oust me from the moment you heard about me."

"Guilty as charged. It was fun."

Was it? It was adrenaline-inducing, painful at times, and, yeah... kind of fun. I like *this*, though. This is nicer. Ryan types around on the iPad, probably sending himself a memo of my suggestions. Finally, he sets the iPad down, draining his glass of wine.

As he reaches for the bottle, I have other ideas. Setting my glass beside his, I slide off the couch, landing on my knees beside his leg. Ryan pauses, glancing at me with surprise, his arm still outstretched toward the wine bottle. Placing a hand on his chest, I gently shove him backward. He wouldn't move if he didn't want to, but he helpfully sits back, his arm dropping to the couch beside him as I bat my lashes, looking up at him through them and sinking my teeth into my lower lip.

Ryan's pupils dilate again as I slide his zipper down, reaching into his jeans and caressing his cock.

"What do you plan to do with that?"

Hold My Heart

Damn, he's so cocky. It should annoy me, but it's turning me on. He has every right to be cocky. Once upon a time, that would have bugged me, but not right now. I throw him a knowing look, lifting his cock out of his jeans and lowering my head.

"Yeah, do that," he groans as my lips close around the head. I remember to wrap my teeth behind my lips, so I don't graze him and start bobbing, sucking, and swallowing.

"Fuck, Layla. That feels amazing, babe."

Keeping that feedback in mind – I always was good at following instructions – I keep my rhythm and tempo, reaching into his jeans with my other hand to massage his balls, which draws a long, low groan out of him. It rumbles right out of his chest. I have him exactly where I want him.

Swirling my tongue around, I cram as much of his cock into my mouth as I can, wrapping my remaining hand around the base of the shaft and working it in time with my bobbing motions.

"Yes, babe. *Ye-es.*" Ryan comes with a grunt, and I quickly swallow. Licking my lips, my hand slides out of his jeans as I move to ensure my face isn't a mess and sit back on my heels. Ryan's face is flushed, and his eyes are bright as he stares at me.

"Now, *that's* a way to end a brainstorming session."

Yeah. It is.

K.S. ELLIS

Chapter Sixteen

Ryan

My eyes flicker over Layla, who is staring, mesmerized, as the lights wink on across the city. I like the view up here, and this time of day is amazing, but looking at it through Layla's eyes is…nice. I wasn't exactly getting inoculated to it – it's hard to get inoculated to *this* view – but maybe I wasn't quite as captivated by it lately. There's that saying about seeing the world through a child's eyes, but I don't need to watch a kid look at things. I'd rather watch Layla. It's cute the way her face lights up when she sees something like this view. Like she's watching magic.

Smiling at the sight of her, I finish plating up the dinner I ordered and take it over to where she's perched at the outdoor bar. I was going to set up the meal downstairs, but then I remembered how eagerly she asked if we were going to the roof. David's wife, Ani, is obsessed with their rooftop terrace overlooking Central Park in New York. A little like Layla is here. It's cute.

When I set the plates down, Layla tears her eyes away from the city, smiling up at me. "Thanks, this smells amazing."

"I have this restaurant on speed dial. They do the best semolina gnocchi known to man."

"That's a big call," she teases. I tap my wine glass against hers and nod at her plate.

"Take a bite and tell me I'm wrong."

Giggling, Layla spears a piece of gnocchi and Italian sausage. The fork disappears into the glorious mouth that had my cock in it less than two hours ago, and I watch her eyes flutter closed with pleasure. I told her it was the best.

Layla's eyes fly open, and she grins at me. "I've never had semolina gnocchi before, so I can't say it's the *best*. But it's pretty amazing."

Rolling my eyes, I laugh, forking my own mouthful in. It is the best. It melts on your tongue. I eat this *way* too frequently, which is probably why I keep a fully stocked home gym next to the garage. Savoring the delicious taste of my food, I enjoy watching Layla eat. She eats like she looks at my view – with wonder. It's making my cock hard. Again. Greedy little bastard.

My eyes linger on her weird dress with the ruffle at the chest and the light and dark purple stripes. The sleeves come to her wrists and the neckline to her collarbones. It's... so prissy it almost hurts to look at. How the *fuck* is it sexy? It's Layla. It has to be Layla. She sucked me off looking like a

Victorian nanny. I think my brain is broken, and I'm getting off that shit.

Before all this business with her, my go-to was supermodels. I haven't had a date in months, and I haven't even fucking noticed. The words are out of my mouth before I realize what I'm saying. "Come to the Symposium in Philadelphia with me."

Layla blinks, her glass of wine frozen halfway to her mouth.

"The one next week?" She looks so adorably confused.

"Yeah. That one. I can't think of another one coming up in Philly."

Layla doesn't roll her eyes, which is her go-to move when she thinks I'm being a cocky bastard. Instead, she takes a sip of her wine, carefully setting it down on the bar like she's contemplating her next words carefully. I shift in my seat. Am I nervous? About what the woman is going to fucking say? I've never been nervous about a woman responding to me asking her anywhere. Granted, they usually say yes, but I've had the occasional rejection before, and it's never bothered me.

Would it bother me if Layla said no? Why? Because it's Layla? Because I'm me and she's her, and I think she should jump at this chance?

"I'd love to come. It'd be great to see how one is run. I'll have Karly organize my room. She can liaise with Andy to ensure we're in the same hotel."

Nodding, I pluck up my wine and take a sip, the taste tangy and bitter on my tongue. It didn't taste like that the last sip I had. She's coming. But she's planning to stay in a different hotel room. Why? Why wouldn't she stay in my suite? What the fuck is happening right now?

Layla

Ryan nods, draining his wine. Well, I suppose ending on a professional note is probably smart. He did ask me over here to work out a professional issue. All other… extra-curricular activities aside, I'm glad we ended here. Setting my empty glass down, I slide off the bar stool – still not gracefully – and collect my purse.

"Dinner was amazing. I'm sure you're right – the best semolina gnocchi there is."

Ryan grins, also standing and escorting me downstairs. He's tapping on his phone as we walk, probably ordering me a town car. Huh, maybe he is more of a gentleman than I have previously given him credit for. He's certainly never left me to make my own way home.

As we reach the front door, he spins me around, his hands coming up to cup my face and his lips crashing down on mine. Okay, so not a totally professional note to end things on, but definitely my favorite goodbye that he gives. I moan, letting his tongue dance its way into my mouth and tango with mine until he lifts his head – always too soon – grinning at me.

"Your chariot awaits."

Ugh. I can't tell if he's being corny or teasing. My cheeks flush, and I giggle, doing a weird, random, *badly executed* curtsey and hurrying out the door as Ryan's laughter follows me.

The driver holds the door open, and I don't bother to look over. Ryan will be long gone. Instead, I dig my phone out of my purse, googling the Philadelphia Symposium. A week. Wow. Okay. I shoot Karly a detailed email, telling her to liaise with Andy and book me on the same flights and in the same hotel as Ryan. I have bigger fish to fry. If we're flying out tomorrow or Monday, I need to pack and ensure that my wardrobe is on point. I'm going to be representing Haven Pharmaceuticals. This is big. Okay. I need not to hyperventilate. And I need to call Allison.

K.S. Ellis

Chapter Seventeen

Ryan

My eyes are glued to the back of Layla's head as she shifts slightly in her stance, still tapping at her phone. Her feet hurt. That's why she can't stand still. I don't blame them for hurting. She's wearing six-inch heels. I'm surprised she hasn't face-planted. I think her lack of height bothers her. It doesn't bother me. I like picking her up to kiss her properly. It keeps all that jasmine-smelling goodness pressed against me. Right where I want it.

My fingers itch to touch her, but I don't, raising my eyebrows and nodding as the elevator doors open, and she turns with a smile. "You were right. The jerk chicken was amazing. Thanks for dinner. I'll see you in the lobby tomorrow to get a cab together?"

"Have a good night, Layla."

The doors close as she turns and walks off, and I let out the sigh I was holding. Being uber professional and not touching was *not* what I had in mind when I invited her to this thing. I imagined a lot more stolen kisses, sweaty limbs, and tangled sheets. My plans were a lot more fun than this is turning out to be. Don't get me wrong. It's been fun hanging out with Layla and watching her master the industry. She's a quick study, and she's a people person. Watching her work a room is ridiculously sexy. But watching her work a room in her prissy clothes, knowing the lacy lingerie that is likely to be hidden under them, is torture. Pure torture.

The elevator dings, and I step out onto the plush carpet of the penthouse floor. I get halfway down the hallway before my fingers work the knot of my tie, loosening it and moving to shove through my hair. Fuck this.

Turning, I stride back to the elevator, jabbing the down button. It hasn't left since I got out, and the doors immediately slide open. Perfect. Stepping inside, I hit the button for Layla's floor and the close doors button incessantly until they finally shut. It feels like an age until the doors ping, and I slide out before they're even fully open, making my way down the hallway until I reach the door I'm looking for. Letting out a long breath, I raise my hand and knock.

"Just a second!" she calls from inside. It better only be a second. I'm going out of my mind here.

The door opens, and Layla blinks at me. She's shorter now, having removed those torture devices she had strapped to her feet. "Ryan, did you forget something?"

"Yeah," I growl at her, crowding her until I'm in the room, kicking the door shut behind me. Layla blinks up at me, her voice breathier than before.

HOLD MY HEART

"And what's that?"

"To fuck you into your mattress and then rub your feet. They're sore."

"They are sore," Layla sighs as my mouth crashes down on hers. Grabbing her ass, I lift her, walking us through the room to the bed. Layla giggles as I drop her onto the bed, taking a seat and picking up her foot.

"I thought the foot massage was coming after?" she laughs, her giggles cutting out as I start firmly working the base of her foot with my thumbs.

Yeah, it was. But they're sore *now*. Besides, I don't intend to leave this room until morning, so there's plenty of time for sex. Layla's eyes flutter closed as she moans softly, each sound like a lightning bolt to my aching cock. Oh, why the fuck did no one ever tell me that giving a foot massage was foreplay?

Layla peeks through her eyelids, offering me a sexy smile. "Sex after, right?"

Chuckling, I wink at her. "How about when you're ready for the massage to be over, you start touching yourself. I might be a clueless male, but I don't think I'll miss *that* hint."

Layla rolls her eyes, even as they flutter shut, a loud moan ripping through her when I press a firm circle against the pad of her left foot. I shift uncomfortably, gritting my teeth and focusing on giving the best damn foot massage I've ever done in my life. And also the first.

Finally, Layla's foot feels less tense as I rub it, and I switch to her right one. She lets out another loud moan, but I'm ready this time, ignoring my greedy cock twitching in my pants. I don't blame the twitchy bastard. This is a glorious sight. Layla is spread out before me, sprawled across the bed. Her hair has come loose from her updo and lies across the pillow, her limbs floppy.

Layla moves from her comfortable position of repose as I itch to stretch my thumbs. The only part of her that moves is her right arm, from laying on the bed to resting on her leg. I glance at her face, but her eyes are still closed, enjoying my foot rub. My eyes move back to her hand, glued to it as it creeps closer to her crotch. She tugs up her floaty skirt, exposing white lacy panties. My tongue darts out at the sight. White lacy panties? Why did I expect anything else from my prissy Ms. Hall?

My mouth is dry, my thumbs getting a new lease on life, still massaging as my eyes watch her fingers creep into her panties, parting her folds and circling her clit. Yeah. Definitely a glorious sight. I let her work her clit, enjoying the show. Out of the corner of my eye, Layla's eyelid crack a tiny bit. Just to check that I got the hint. Oh yeah, I got the hint.

HOLD MY HEART

Smirking, I drop her foot, stripping off my tie and jacket as I crawl up the bed, tearing off her panties and knocking her fingers aside, replacing them with my mouth.

"Yes, Ryan," Layla gasps, wrapping her legs around my head. I'm happy to oblige, flicking her clit with my tongue as I kick off my shoes. She's already primed with her finger work, knowing I was watching her, so Layla tumbles over the edge quickly as I lick her clit. As soon as her thighs stiffen and shake, I kiss my way up her body, stripping off her dress and the rest of my clothes as I go.

Hovering over her, I grin, hooking her legs over my hips and grabbing her as I roll us over until she's straddling me. Layla's eyes widen, and she smiles down at me. "You're surrendering control? How... big of you."

Bucking my hips, I press my hard cock up against her core. "I'll show you big."

"Yeah, you will."

Layla's tone cuts from teasing to breathy as she reaches down, caressing my cock. She positions it and sinks down until I'm fully sheathed. A groan rips out of me. Fuck, she feels amazing.

I stretch my arms behind my head, watching Layla with amusement as she sighs, opening her eyes glazed with pleasure.

"What?" she asks, sounding both amused and turned on.

"I'm intrigued with what you're going to do with all this power I'm allowing you."

Layla grins, swiveling her hips and leaning forward until her lips brush mine. "Oh, Ryan. This isn't the first time I've had all the power."

What? "Is that so?"

"Remember when I sucked your cock?"

My hips buck involuntarily as I remember that Victorian nanny outfit. Fuck yeah, I do. That was so good I lost my head and invited her this week, so I could have more of it.

"It rings a bell."

"I had *all* the power."

Yeah. She fucking did. How about that? "Okay. Let's see if you can make this as good as that was."

Layla snaps upright, gasping in mock outrage as her hands land on my pecs, steadying herself.

"Challenge accepted, Mr. Pierce Westerhaven."

Oh no, she didn't. "It's. Ryan."

I have to grit my teeth to get it out because Layla decides to swivel her hips and clench her inner muscles as I speak. What are those exercises called? Kegels or something? I bet Layla does that because she has phenomenal control.

"Shit, babe."

"All the power, Ryan. Remember that."

"Do you want me to surrender or something?"

HOLD MY HEART

Layla grins, still swiveling and clenching. "No. I just want you to remember it."

"I don't think I'll forget this any time soon, babe."

"Good." There's a glint of a challenge in Layla's eye, and I am ready to white-knuckle this ride, hanging on for dear life. Bring it.

Bracing against my chest, Layla stops swiveling, bouncing on my cock instead. She might not be swiveling anymore, but she's still rhythmically clenching at my cock with her pussy muscles as she bounces. My eyes are almost rolling back in my head. Fuck. I hope she comes soon because I am and don't know if I can be a gentleman with this action.

"Layla, I'm close."

"Good."

Fuck. I'm fucking screwed. Ah well, she came before, and I'll have her screaming my name sometime throughout the night. Plus, I have the rest of this week. Layla catches me off guard, clenching hard and swiveling mid-bounce.

"Fuck!" I hiss, my hips bucking as I come. Layla slides off me with a giggle, curling up against my side with a smug smile. She should be cocky. That was incredible. Layla's lips tickle my chest as she speaks, still snuggled against me.

"Isn't this about when you should look for your pants?"

I tip my head forward, grinning at her. "Oh, babe, I'm not going anywhere...except to hit the lights. How can I taste you again tonight if I'm in another room?"

Layla stares, blinking, though I catch a hint of a small smile as I slide out of bed to turn off the lights and set the "Do Not Disturb" sign on the door.

Layla

Blinking awake, I stretch, my hand making contact with flesh. A grunt rings out, and I glance over with a grimace. Oops. Ryan rubs his chin, opening bleary eyes and blinking at me.

"Is there a reason I just got clocked in the jaw?"

"Uh, I forgot you were here and stretched?"

Ryan growls, then grins, rolling over and nuzzling his nose against my neck. "I think we can help you remember for the rest of the week."

What? What does that mean? "Are you planning on moving in here or something?"

Ryan lifts his head, looking around the hotel room. I follow his gaze. This room is similar to the one I had in

HOLD MY HEART

Chicago for my four-day job interview. It's high ceilings, huge bed, and small couch scream *fancy*. He snorts, turning back to me and deliberately rolling his eyes. Hey. That's *my* move.

"This place is tiny. We would drive each other insane in a day."

Tiny? This room is *huge*. Also, if he's not moving in here, I'm confused about what he meant about helping me remember he's in my bed. Ryan peppers my throat with kisses. "I have a suite. You're moving in. Pack your stuff."

Uh, what? "Pack my stuff? Is that an order?"

"Yeah."

"What happened to me having all the power?"

With a chuckle, Ryan rolls on top of me, his cock prodding my entrance. My thighs spread, hugging the side of his hips of their own volition.

"You have all the power when my cock is in your mouth or if you're on top. Are either of those things happening right now?"

I'm about to answer when the words are robbed from my mouth, nothing but a breathy sigh coming out as Ryan sinks into me, stretching me gloriously.

"Are they?"

"No," I whisper, my eyes fluttering closed on Ryan's triumphant smirk as he thrusts into me.

"I didn't think so. When we're done here, pack your things and bring them up."

"Okay." I blame his cock. It's moving inside me, filling all the space and driving me out of my mind. I'm hardly about to turn down the offer of this every morning we are here, simply to make a point about him "ordering" it. Ryan's hand slips under my ass, gripping it as he changes the angle. Hmm, maybe I should have held out, and he might have spanked me again. On second thoughts, perhaps I'll keep that in my arsenal for another time. This is just as good an incentive.

Chapter Eighteen

Layla

Standing in front of my closet, my cheeks flame as I pick out an outfit for tomorrow. Normally this wouldn't be so... blush-worthy. But I'm not just laying out an outfit for tomorrow. My overnight bag is sitting in the middle of my bed. Everything else is packed, just waiting for my clothes.

Since we came home from the symposium in Philadelphia a few weeks ago, Ryan has been inviting me over after work. And I've been staying the night. Waking up to that view is... everything. Having Ryan sleeping in the bed next to me is pretty nice too. But then I have to come home, get ready, and get to work. It's been exhausting. Also, I've been waking up early and effectively sneaking out. It's obviously been bugging Ryan because instead of walking me to his fancy SUV, he told me to pack an overnight bag and meet at his. So it's not a spontaneous sleepover. This is... different. Hence the blushes.

My hands land on two different outfits. I don't know which one I want to wear. I sneak a peek at the clock on my nightstand. Crap. I need to pick. I need to call the town car.

Sighing, I grab them both, carefully folding them into the overnight bag and adding shoes for each. I'll choose tomorrow morning. I'll have so much time. And I'll get to use that shower. I think I'm looking forward to that more than anything else. Pulling up the town car app that Ryan loaded on my phone last week, I order one, grab my overnight bag and purse, and make my way downstairs to collect a nice bottle of wine I picked over the weekend. And the cookies I baked yesterday.

I tuck them both into my purse, stepping outside as the town car pulls up. The driver holds open the door, and I slide in. Is it just me, or is he looking at my overnight bag? No. I need to get out of my head. I pull out my phone to distract myself, tapping around my emails. Ryan always invites me over to debrief any issues that arise throughout the day. I don't know if that's cover or if he needs that, because this is just a workplace hookup for him. Whatever it is, I'm going to be prepared. I can't help it. I like it when he looks impressed at my work knowledge.

"We're here, Ms. Hall."

Shoving my phone into my purse, I seize it and my overnight bag, sliding out and ringing the doorbell. Ryan opens the door, his eyes landing on my bag as he grins.

"I'll take that."

HOLD MY HEART

I surrender the overnight bag, following him up to the middle level. He takes my things into his bedroom, through the bathroom, and into the walk-in closet to die for. There's a plush bench seat in the middle of it! This can't be a real house. Ryan points to a kind of bare section in between all his neatly pressed shirts, pants, and suit jackets.

"I cleared a space for your clothes for tomorrow."

My cheeks heat at the implication, but Ryan doesn't notice, turning out of the room. "I'll start plating up dinner upstairs when you're all settled in."

I stare after him as he leaves. Just like that, huh? Swallowing, I open my overnight bag and lift out both outfits, carefully hanging them to ensure there are no wrinkles from their travels and setting both pairs of shoes on the rack below them. There's also an empty shelf, so I unpack my underwear and blush as I place the silky pajamas there too.

I usually sleep naked – obviously – but I thought, why not? Stowing the empty bag on another shelf in the "cleared" section, I take my makeup, jewelry, and toiletries bags into the bathroom, swallowing again at the empty vanity drawer that sits open. Ryan must have pulled it out for me on his way through. This is… intimate. Don't overthink it, Layla! I drop my bags into the drawer, shove it closed and hurry out of the room.

Snatching up my purse from the bed, I make my way to the living room. Ryan is standing at the huge black marble-topped kitchen island, plating the takeaway onto fancy dinnerware. I don't know if Ryan knows how to cook, but he never seems to. I should offer to make dinner for him one night. I'm a decent cook. I can do all the staples, and I don't know how often he gets a home cooked meal.

I set my purse on the sideboard, removing the container of cookies and the wine bottle. Ryan's eyes linger on the container. "What's that?"

"Uh, oatmeal raisin cookies." My cheeks flame as his eyebrows shoot up.

"What store? I don't think I've ever seen packaging like that before."

He sounds dubious. Okay, so my reusable container has a few years of lunch mileage. It's not *that* bad. "Uh, my oven?"

Ryan's frown deepens. "Is that in Encino?"

I giggle. Oh my god. He's so adorably clueless. Crossing to him, I set both items on the island and flip open the container. "I made them, genius."

Ryan's face immediately clears, and he grins at the cookies. "You bake?"

"I can make oatmeal raisin cookies."

"Hey, why branch out when you can absolutely nail something."

HOLD MY HEART

Yeah. I figured that too. Ryan's eyes linger on the cookies as he finishes plating up the salmon polpette and herb linguine. It smells mouthwatering. I take the plates to the glass-topped table beside the lounge area, its hanging pendant lighting illuminating the space, the lights of LA *right there* beside the table. Amazing.

Ryan follows with my wine and two glasses. I blush. "I'm sure you have something that pairs better."

He shakes his head, pouring two glasses before taking his seat across from me. "This is oak-aged Chardonnay. It will pair beautifully."

Oh? Go me. I take a sip, twirling the linguine around my fork as Ryan flashes me a grin. "What did you think of the latest beta version of the expiry date software?"

I knew he was taking as much of an interest in that as I was. I mean, it's kind of... our baby, in a way. Is it weird to think of it like that?

"I think we're getting close."

"Yeah, we're definitely on the right track with it."

Nodding, I take a mouthful of linguine, my eyes fluttering closed. Ryan always knows the most perfect meals to order. When I open my eyes, my cheeks flame as my gaze lands on Ryan, watching me with a smile.

"What are you thinking?" I ask, my eyes narrowing with suspicion. Why is he smiling at me like that?

"That I'm going to eat a cookie after we finish here, and then I'm going to lay you out on this table and have you for dessert."

"O-okay." My mouth is dry. That's definitely a nice thought.

Ryan

Wedging my phone between my ear and shoulder, I fix my cufflinks and walk into the closet, searching for my tie.

"You're going to the opera? Seriously?" David snorts. I roll my eyes.

"Lucas's wife loves it. They invite me every year."

"You don't have to say yes, you know."

No, I don't. But that would insult Lucas, which I don't want to do, and besides... I don't mind the opera. "Whatever, dude. At least I'm getting out of the house. When was the last time you saw sunlight with your two rugrats."

"Tell me, what's the background picture on your phone right now?"

Busted. "Your rugrats."

HOLD MY HEART

"Ooh, they've knocked little William from the pride of place?"

"He's my home screen."

David continues to crow about how he's going to lord it over Timmy that his kids have the picture on my lock screen. My eyes land on my tie, and I pluck it up, half-listening to David's smug monologue. I'm distracted by another sight here in my closet. The space I cleared for Layla to leave her work clothes when she stays the night. It's not empty. She's been bringing an overnight bag for the last two weeks, but apparently, she's not taking everything with her.

Two prissy dresses are hanging over two pairs of her weird shoes. One is the strappy heels, and the other is a Victorian-style pair of heels, like little fancy boots.

"Uh-huh," I murmur into the phone when it sounds like David might be finishing his crowing. It's enough to keep him going as I stare at the clothes. Biting my lower lip to stop smiling, I leave the closet, my eyes finding the clothes one last time as I flip off the lights. She's leaving clothes here? That's... interesting.

Putting the phone on speaker, I drop it on the gray marble vanity, fixing my tie. I have to know. Snagging the handle of the drawer I cleared, I tug it open, the corners of my lips twitching into a smug grin at the sight of a toothbrush, hairbrush, and some makeup. I guess clothes aren't the only thing Layla has been leaving here.

Reaching down, I pluck up her toothbrush, set it in the holder beside mine on the vanity, and finish fixing my tie. My eyes linger on the pair of toothbrushes. Am I losing my mind? I don't think so, but maybe. Shaking my head, I grab my phone, take it off speaker, and turn, flipping off the light. "Maybe I'll mix it up and have William on my lock screen next week."

"Like fuck you will," David chokes, fuming at me as I laugh.

"I have to go. The town car is almost here."

"I'll send you the cutest photo. There's no way William will be able to top it."

"Later, dude."

Hanging up, I drop my phone into my pocket as it starts to buzz. I need to remember to put it on silent. David will be spamming me with cute pictures of his kids all night. That's adorable. At least it will take my mind off why I wasn't annoyed at Layla's things being in my house. I've never let any woman leave things here before. It should bother me. It should bother me that it doesn't bother me.

Chapter Nineteen

Ryan

Waving Andy off, I start on the sushi he brought for lunch, my fingers closing around my phone when it buzzes. Uncle Bill. Shit. Dropping my chopsticks, I swipe to answer, lifting the phone to my ear.

"Ryan. I just saw the profit report. I guess all the changes there in LA are having a positive effect."

You know, even two months ago, that would have disturbed me. Most of those changes are off the back of Layla's solutions. Now? Not so much. We're working as a well-oiled machine. Why would that annoy me?

"Ms. Hall is a good addition to the team here. I commend you on your choice."

Uncle Bill chuckles. He probably remembers my phone call when I discovered that Layla was the new COO and my fury. Well, I've learned a thing or two since then, including just how to get the best out of Layla's brilliant mind.

"I knew she would fit well."

"She certainly fits well."

I'm not thinking about Layla's position at Haven Pharmaceuticals right now. I'm thinking about her writhing in front of me as I plow into her. She fits *very* well. Shit. Uncle Bill is talking again. I shift in my seat to relieve some of the pressure of my now-hard cock straining against my fly. I need to pay attention.

"I'm attending the pharmaceutical conference in DC next week. I believe both Ms. Hall and you are attending?"

"That's correct. Andy has already booked the flights and hotel."

He's booked a single suite. I haven't discussed it with Layla, but I think she will be amenable to sharing with me. I think it will be the most pleasurable conference I've ever attended.

"Good. I'll have Cathy liaise with Andy and Ms. Hall's assistant to organize a dinner the night I arrive."

"I look forward to it, and I'm sure Ms. Hall feels the same."

"Good. Good. It will be interesting to see the two of you interact. Lucas has led me to believe there were initially fireworks when Ms. Hall started."

Is that a remonstration in his tone? Fuck. "Some settling in issues. Nothing serious."

"I'm sure."

At least he sounds amused now. I hang up, scoffing my sushi and standing. I'll have to give Layla a heads-up that Uncle Bill will join us. I smirk at the thought of seeing Layla interact with him. She kept calling me "Mr. Pierce Westerhaven" when she first arrived. I wonder if she's going to show Uncle Bill the same deference. I wonder if he'll let her.

Layla

There is a throat clearing, and I glance up from my salad. Ryan is standing in the doorway, leaning against it, his hands in his pocket.

"Knock knock."

"Oh, sorry. Karly went to get some new stationery for the DC trip."

His eyebrows shoot up. "You're buying new stationery to take to a conference?"

"I might want to take notes."

His eyes drift over my checkered pinafore. "Will it match your outfits?"

I bristle at his teasing and match his smile. Two can play that game, and Ryan needs to remember that I can give as well as I get. "No. It's going to match my lingerie underneath."

Ryan's lips part, and his pupils dilate. My breath catches at the sight. In the past, a look like that has led to some sneaky office sex. Sadly, not today. Ryan leaves the door open – boo – as he strolls across the room, around the desk, and leans over my shoulder, his breath tickling my neck.

"That's a brilliant idea. I look forward to it."

Shit. We're playing with fire now. Karly could come back at any moment – and I still haven't told her I'm sleeping with Ryan. It felt a bit personal. I quickly change the subject to safer ground.

"Karly said Andy insisted on booking everything for me in DC when he booked yours."

"Well, I thought you might not want it common knowledge that we're sharing a suite."

My heart thuds in my chest. I had wondered after Philadelphia, and that I sleep at his house every second or third night, if we would be staying together. But confirmation... it's stomach fluttering.

"You thought right."

"I've also booked us to arrive the Friday before."

"Why?"

"I wanted a weekend in DC with you before reality intruded. Is that okay?"

Screw fluttering. My stomach is in knots. Oh my. That's... wow.

Hold My Heart

"More than okay."

Ryan chuckles, straightening and smirking down at me. "Good, because I'm about to burst that bubble."

Wh-what? "O...kay?"

"Uncle Bill will be joining us in DC. He'll arrive on Monday, and we'll have dinner with him that night."

Bill... Westerhaven? Oh. *Oh.* Ryan grins as he watches the emotions wash over my face. Asshole.

"And we're still sharing a suite after you knew he was coming?"

Ryan's eyebrows shoot up. "Uh, yes. He's not coming to the suite with us. He won't know."

Okay. That's... okay. I nod jerkily. "If Mr. Westerhaven is going to be there, I need to rethink my wardrobe."

Ryan is grinning for some reason. "At least you won't have to change your stationery order. The only person seeing your lingerie will be me."

My eyes snap to his, my cheeks heating as his eyes promise me a hell of a good time. Yes, *please.* That's exactly what I need to distract me from my panic about attending a conference with Mr. Westerhaven. I can't put a foot wrong. I need him to know he made the right choice to place me here. I need to prove his confidence in me wasn't misplaced.

K.S. ELLIS

Chapter Twenty

Layla

The bellhop opens the double doors to our suite with a flourish, wheeling in the bags as Ryan's hand lands on my lower back. He guides me inside with a smile, and it takes every ounce of self-control I have not to gape like a fish. This is not a hotel suite. This is... a palace. We're in a foyer. *Inside* our suite. There are fancy waiting stools. And palm trees. I think Ryan has stayed here before because he knows where he's going. He guides me through the living room with a fireplace and a freaking *chess set*.

My heels tap over the white marble floors as we move through the, I guess... library, with a polished wood desk and a huge TV unit. Finally, we arrive at the bedroom, bigger than my living room back in LA. Ryan's suite in Philadelphia was nice, but it had nothing on this. I don't know if he always travels like this, or if it's because he's impressing me... if it's that, I'm very impressed.

I want to run and jump onto the huge king bed to see if I bounce and if it's as soft as it looks. But the bellhop is still here, waiting for Ryan to subtly slip him a tip as they shake hands. That's so cool. I want to learn how to do that. It's such a rich people way to tip.

As the bellhop leaves, I turn to Ryan, waggling my eyebrows. "This place is so fancy. I'm surprised there isn't a dining room."

Ryan glances over from where he's moving the bags into the small walk-in closet to start hanging his suits. "There is. It's on the other side of the foyer."

Of course, there is. I bite back a nervous giggle, moving to hang my clothes up and fill the drawers. I'm surprised when Ryan quickly finishes his unpacking and starts to leave.

"You're not going to stay and watch me unpack my lingerie?"

Ryan waggles his eyebrows back at me. "I want them to be a surprise every day when I unwrap you."

I giggle in astonishment as he leaves, continuing to unpack. I'm very careful as I lay out my lingerie in the drawer. I have brought a new pair for each day, just for Ryan. I like the idea of him getting excited about seeing them. He might want to pretend I don't have all the power, but sometimes, I totally do.

I smooth my skirt, checking my hair and makeup in the floor-length mirror in the closet after the long flight. Ryan said something about going out for dinner, and I want to look my best. Maybe it's silly, but I'm nervous. This is just like a couple's vacation. I don't know what that means or if I'm reading too much into this, but I can't help it. It's probably the stupidest thing I've ever done, but I'm falling for Ryan.

With my head on a swivel, taking everything in again as I make my way back to the living area, I smile at Ryan, where he's seated on the couch, his feet propped up on the coffee table as he taps out emails on his phone. Ryan lifts his eyes, flickering over my outfit.

"Are you ready for some sightseeing and dinner?"

"Yes."

Ryan stands, grinning as he shoves his phone into his pocket, and holds out his hand to me.

"And are you ready to come all over that bed after dinner?"

My cheeks flame. He certainly has a way with words. "Yes."

Ryan's hand slides down my back, cupping my ass as he guides me out of the room. "Are you going to wear your sexy lingerie under all your prissy work clothes at the conference?"

Prissy work clothes? I guess I have a certain style. He's never complained about it. And I know he likes my sexy lingerie, whatever he thinks about my other clothes.

"Every. Single. Day."

Ryan's lips quirk, and his eyes sparkle as he leads me out of the room. Yeah, I hold crazy amounts of power, and he doesn't even know it.

Ryan

The walk-in closet door creaks open, and Layla walks out, covered from neck to wrists in her prissy dress. Sliding off the bed, I cross to her, brushing a kiss over her lips as my hands slide down to cup her ass.

"I'm intrigued about what lingerie is under here," I murmur. Layla looks up at me through her long, dark lashes.

"You'll just have to wait and see."

She grins, stepping away from me. Uh, I can't wait. I follow her out of the room, guiding her to the lobby and outside, where our car is waiting. The conference isn't far from our hotel and doesn't take long to get to. Layla follows me inside, smiling as we stop to register and collect our lanyards. Layla hooks hers over her head and grins at me.

"Are you ready?" I waggle my eyebrows at her, and Layla's eyes narrow suspiciously.

Hold My Heart

"This will be different from the symposium, won't it?"

"Uh, yeah."

"Why do you say it like that?"

She's right to be suspicious. "The symposium was more about sharing new products and ideas. This is more... networking."

"Okay. You're still saying it weird."

"Some people at stuff like this are... a lot."

Layla doesn't look like she believes me. Oh boy, is she in for a ride. We follow the crowd into the large ballroom, where the rows of chairs are neatly lined up. Layla trails me into the seats reserved for us near the front row. I nod to Josh Burnett from Burnett Pharmaceuticals, who is taking his seat across the aisle. He returns my nod, sitting and turning his attention to the stage. Burnett Pharmaceuticals, also based in LA, is one of our biggest competitors. Josh doesn't run the company. That is his father's job. But Josh is the head of their acquisitions arm. We don't have an acquisitions arm, focusing instead on our own R&D.

I'm distracted from Josh Burnett's presence as Layla digs through her purse and pulls out a little pink notepad and pen with a pink and gold design. My eyes drink in the notepad and pen, and I remember her saying she was matching it to her lingerie. Does that mean she's wearing pink lingerie? I fucking hope so. That color would look damn good on her. My mouth is watering at the thought.

But also.... "Why do you have a notepad and pen?"

Layla glances at me in surprise. "Uh, to take notes from the presentation."

That's cute. Grinning, I pat her hand. "It's not that kind of presentation."

Layla looks confused, but her face disappears from view as the lights cut out.

"Uh...." she whispers, falling silent as the light show starts. These things are always so over the top. The announcer is blaring over the rock music, but I'm more interested in using this helpful darkness to enlighten myself further on Layla's lingerie. My fingers skate her leg, ignoring her squirming and her hands trying to brush me off. When I hit bare leg, she freezes. I don't even know if she's breathing, her eyes glued to the stage where the first speaker emerges from the dry ice clouds.

I hook my fingers up until I brush lace. Fuck. She's wearing a garter belt. Best. Conference. *Ever*. Layla squirms, and I take pity on her, removing my hand – also for my own sake. If I keep my hand in there, I won't be able to wait until after this presentation is over.

The lights come back up, and I glance at Layla, smirking at the shellshocked look on her face.

"Why do I feel like I've just attended a heavy metal concert?"

"The ringing disappears after an hour or so."

She giggles, standing when I do. We reach the aisle at the same time as Josh Burnett, who smiles and gallantly gestures for Layla to precede him. He nods to me, moving off and chatting with his companion. I have other things on my mind. Sliding my hand up Layla's back, I move us away from the crowd heading to various coffee events before the first speaker events start.

"Uh, we're supposed to be in conference room -"

Layla cuts off as I open the door to a janitor's closet, hustling her inside.

"This is not conference room six," she observes drily.

"No, it's not. We'll get there in a minute."

"Just a minute?"

Oh, she's going to pay for that. Layla giggles as my lips trail up her throat, and I gently push her against the shelving, stepping back to lift her poodle skirt. Oh yeah. There's that cotton candy pink garter belt I was hoping to see.

"I knew it," I breathe. Layla giggles, biting her lower lip as I growl, closing the distance between us and hooking her legs over my hips as I free my cock. It springs out of my pants, rubbing against that tantalizing lace.

Layla moans with anticipation. Same, babe. Same. Shoving her panties aside, I plunge into her wet heat, capturing her lips to swallow her moans. We are in a janitor's closet. We have to be kinda quiet. Layla's fingers dig into my shoulders as I hammer into her.

"Are you gonna come for me, babe?"

"Yes," she whispers against my lips, her hips straining forward as I pick up the pace.

"Good girl," I grunt. Layla's pussy spasms as she comes with a breathy moan. That's what I was waiting for. Continuing to hammer into her, I groan my release, panting against her neck.

"Shall we get to our first speaker event?"

Layla's breath shudders out of her as I set her down, tucking my cock away while she straightens her outfit.

"I'm ready when you are."

My lips stretch into a smile. Sometimes I forget just what a match for me Layla is. I never want to lose sight of that.

Chapter Twenty-One

Ryan

Layla smooths her skirt and fidgets with her bracelet as I guide her into the restaurant. Her head is on a swivel as the white-jacketed waiters move around silently.

"Mr. Westerhaven is seated through here," the hostess informs us as she leads us through the busy restaurant. Sure enough, Uncle Bill is seated in the furthermost corner of the room, half-hidden behind a large palm frond. He's never felt comfortable in the middle of a room, on display.

I usually let them seat me wherever. I've grown up in a fishbowl, so I don't notice it as much these days. Layla is fidgeting again. I don't know if she's nervous about meeting with Uncle Bill or simply nervous about how everyone is sneaking peeks at us as we pass. Uncle Bill rises as we approach, smiling broadly at Layla and greeting her with a kiss on the cheek.

"It's lovely to see you again, Ms. Hall. I'm gratified that you have settled in well at Haven Pharmaceuticals."

"Thank you, Mr. Westerhaven. I'm only glad I could reward your confidence in me."

Taking our seats, Uncle Bill orders wine for the table, and general small talk flows around as we select our menu items and order. As the waiter melts away, Uncle Bill holds his wine glass in a toast toward Layla.

"To Ms. Hall. I am most impressed with the changes at Haven Pharmaceuticals and how it has improved its market share drastically since you came on board."

Layla giggles and blushes as I lift my glass in turn. It's true. Layla's solutions have helped the company go from strength to strength. Well, Layla's solutions with my input and improvements. Let's not forget about that. Recovering from her shyness at the praise being heaped upon her, Layla takes a sip of wine and beams at Uncle Bill.

"I only have you to thank. I wouldn't be here if I hadn't been plucked from obscurity as a junior manager at Haven Freight. I can't thank you enough for the opportunity. I'm thankful I have been able to live up to expectations."

As the conversation continues, Uncle Bill smiles and taps his wine glass against hers. I'm unable to move on with it. She... what? What the fuck is that supposed to mean? She was plucked from obscurity? I vaguely recall using the same words about her at some point, but that was... being facetious.

I know Layla was a junior manager at Haven Freight at some point. After all, that's how you move to senior manager and then to COO. Didn't she apply for the job at Haven

Hold My Heart

Pharmaceuticals that Uncle Bill was putting out feelers for behind my back? The only way she could have been randomly plucked from a junior management pool at a different Haven company is if... fuck my life. She's the woman he picked for me. Isn't she? She's my... Angie, Ani, Sam, Nic, *woman*. She's my setup. Jesus.

No. Uncle Bill wouldn't risk one of his precious companies by placing a random, inexperienced woman as COO. I'm reading into this because fucking Beau got into my head with his matchmaking nonsense. Layla is brilliant at her job. There's no way some random woman Uncle Bill picked for me to marry would be *that good* as COO of a multi-billion-dollar company. There's no way.

Shoving the notion aside, I flash a smile and join in the conversation about the speakers we will be hearing from tomorrow. Uncle Bill is particularly interested in a German pharmacist who has pioneered a new anti-viral drug.

Layla's foot brushes my ankle, and I absentmindedly return the pressure. As much as I want to push the idea that Layla is the woman Uncle Bill picked for me out of my head, it keeps eating at me. It better stop soon. I don't want it to get in the way of enjoying this week with Layla in my hotel bed.

Layla

Accepting the coffee and pastry with a smile, I turn to find Ryan in the crowd. He was weird after dinner two nights ago. I can't describe it. After I met his uncle, it's like he's pulling away from me. I thought he would be fine being together with his uncle here. After all, *he's* the one who suggested we share a suite, and that's *after* he knew his uncle would be joining us. Hell, Ryan acted like *I* would be the one acting weird about it. But it's him!

Maybe he was all gung-ho about it until the situation confronted him. We still have sex every night, but it's been like he was only half there. A little detached, and it made me feel weird. Uncomfortable.

I finally spot him, where he's chatting with another conference attendee, and cross to them, slipping in beside him and joining the conversation. Eventually, Ryan's companion wanders off to get his own food, and I grab Ryan's elbow, half-dragging him out of the room, leaving our empty dishes on one of the many white-clothed tables scattered around, seemingly for that exact purpose.

HOLD MY HEART

Ryan doesn't try to stop me from marching him out of the room and into the janitor's closet we screwed in on the first day. I don't know what has gotten into him, but he's not even making the most of my matching lingerie and stationery! It was supposed to be a cute thing to get him all hot under the collar, and he's not playing along. Not like he did on the first day. It's harshing my buzz.

Closing the door behind us, my hands land on my hips, my eyebrows drawing together, and my lips mashing into a thin line. Ryan shoves one hand in his pocket and the other through his hair, tousling it sexily. Ugh, now is *not* the time to get distracted by his yumminess. I need to know what is going on. I need to know if I have to get my own hotel room.

Ryan glances around, his lips quirking a little, and for the first time in two days, it's a glimpse of the Ryan I was getting used to.

"Interesting conversation location choice."

"Yeah, well, I thought you might not want a lot of spectators for this one."

His eyebrows shoot up, and he frowns. "And why is that?"

Isn't it obvious? "Because I'm about to call you on your crap and figured you might not want an audience to watch you getting dressed down."

He waggles his eyebrows. "Are you going to slap me again? As I remember, the payback was very pleasurable."

Ugh. Why does my Ryan have to come out to play *now*? We need to have this conversation, and that's hard when he's back to normal. I think I'm getting whiplash from the sudden change.

"What's going on with you?"

"I... what do you mean?"

The urge to roll my eyes is riding me hard. "I mean... why are you acting so weird?"

"I'm not acting weird. How am I acting weird?"

Seriously? "Uh, you've been... *weird* since we had dinner with your uncle on Monday night."

"Oh, you mean the dinner where it turns out you and my uncle are much closer than I had previously thought?"

What? Is he serious right now? He's been weird because he thinks I'm tight with his uncle?

"Before tonight, I only met your uncle on *one* four-day trip to Chicago when I was there for my job interview. That's hardly being close to him."

"When did you apply for this job, by the way? I didn't even know it was being advertised. I didn't know anything about it until I returned from Beau's wedding to a new COO fucking up my shit."

HOLD MY HEART

I falter. He didn't know about me? He seemed a little off that first day he came into my office, but I figured that was more about my proposals and less about *me*.

"I-I didn't apply. Not exactly. I was invited to Chicago to present solutions to four pharmaceutical industry-specific issues. I went, I presented, and I went home."

"When?"

"I don't know. Five months ago."

Ryan nods stiffly, looking like he's doing math in his head.

"And you got offered the COO position?"

"Yeah, like a month later. I got called into HR, and they gave me the offer and the contract. I hurled in a trashcan."

There is a hint of a smile at my admission, but his frown is back. "What was your role at Haven Freight immediately before moving to Haven Pharmaceuticals?"

What is this? Twenty questions? Shouldn't he know everything from when the board voted me in?

"I was a junior line manager."

Ryan's eyebrows shoot up. "You moved from a junior line manager at Haven Freight to COO of Haven Pharmaceuticals? Plucked from obscurity indeed."

He doesn't need to be a dick about it. I get that it was an out-of-the-blue career progression, but when that kind of opportunity comes knocking, you don't look a gift horse in the mouth!

"Look. Obviously, Mr. Westerhaven put feelers out or something, and one of my managers thought I'd be a good fit and put my name forward. I got this job because I gave my suggestions to the issues, which were the ones I was hired to implement, by the way. I have no idea why you're acting like a dick and quizzing me like you don't already know all this stuff."

Ryan's mouth drops open, both hands now shoved in his pockets. "Why the fuck would I already know this stuff about you? If I knew it, I wouldn't be asking."

I should walk away. We're both getting annoyed, and this is starting to feel like one of our confrontations when I first came to Haven Pharmaceuticals and not one that ended with him inside me. I should... but that's not in my nature.

"You know all this stuff because it wasn't being hidden. All the board members knew this when they voted me in. I had to answer interview questions and everything."

"I wasn't there when you were voted in. It conveniently happened when I was on leave for a family wedding."

"How is that my problem? How is any of this my problem? I haven't done anything wrong!"

HOLD MY HEART

Ryan blows out a breath, glaring at me as my chest heaves and my fingers clench and unclench. I need not to cry right now. That would be the icing on this shitty cake.

"No. You haven't," he snaps, brushing past me. Okay. What the hell does that mean? I hurry after him. I haven't got the answers I want, so we aren't done here.

Chapter Twenty-Two

Ryan

Pulling out my phone, I text Cathy. She'll know where Uncle Bill is. I don't care that it's not professional. I have to fucking know.

CATHY: He's on floor six. The hotel has kindly set up an office for him in one of the smaller meeting rooms. Room 615.

615, that's all I need to know. Layla slips into the elevator beside me, but I ignore her. I have no idea where she's going, but I'll deal with that later. I need to apologize, but I have to have it out with Uncle Bill first. First, I need to get my head straight with how I will play this, and then I can explain to Layla.

The elevator dings, and the doors slide open as I stride out, intent on finding Room 615 as soon as possible and getting this over with. I don't bother knocking, striding into the room, and letting the door swing shut behind me. It must be one of those controlled close ones because it takes an age before it clicks shut.

HOLD MY HEART

Uncle Bill looks up from the polished conference table, where he's typing on his sleek silver laptop. Closing it, he stands, moving around the table toward me.

"I wasn't expecting you to come up. Aren't the speakers still in session?"

The door finally clicks shut behind me. Now I can let loose. Uncle Bill opens his mouth again, but I beat him to it.

"Am I supposed to marry Layla?"

Uncle Bill blinks at me, his eyes lingering on the door over my shoulder. Yeah, I made sure it's shut. No one is hearing this who shouldn't be.

"I would think that would be a question for you to offer Ms. Hall."

No wonder he's made billions. The man is evasive as fuck when he wants to be.

"I'm offering it to you. Did you make Layla COO of Haven Pharmaceuticals because you're matchmaking again?"

The look of shock on Uncle Bill's face is priceless. His eyes dart to the door again. Seriously. Does he think anyone other than me will barge in here without knocking?

Uncle Bill's gaze lands on me again, his eyes hard. "Ms. Hall was hired into her position because a COO was necessary, and she was qualified for it. If you have any issues regarding Ms. Hall's suitability, I suggest you take it up with the board of Haven Pharmaceuticals. I merely put forth the name of an appropriate candidate. The board took it from there. Whatever you're insinuating, you are smearing several names. Whatever you think of me, my power isn't that great."

Bullshit, it's not. But before I can fire back a response, Uncle Bill stalks past me to the door. I turn to call him out again and find myself face to face with an extremely pale and horrified Layla. Fuck. My. Life. Has she been standing there this whole time? Oh boy, have I fucked up.

Layla

The door swings shut behind Mr. Westerhaven, and time is going too fast and too slow all at once. My heart is thudding loudly in my ears. I think it has migrated to my head. Is that even possible? No. Surely not. I'm not going to cry, and I'm not going to faint. I'm not even going to yell. I have never been so humiliated in my life. The fact that Ryan even *thinks* those things about me... hurts. That he would voice them, to *Mr. Westerhaven*, no less. That's just mortifying.

"Layla," Ryan starts, but I don't want to hear it. I think he's said enough.

HOLD MY HEART

"Did you really just come in here to accuse your uncle of parachuting me into a job I'm unqualified for so I'd marry you?"

Pink blooms across Ryan's creamy cheeks. Well, that's a first. Ryan Pierce Westerhaven is blushing. I didn't think shame was an emotion he was capable of feeling.

"It's not like that. Look, all four of my cousins have married this year, and we think Uncle Bill is setting us up. That's all. It's not that big a deal."

It's not that big a deal. I draw myself up to my full five feet, squaring my shoulders and looking him dead in the eye. When I speak, icicles drip off my voice. If only they were real and could pierce his heart the way his accusations pierced mine.

"So you think I'm unqualified for my job, and the only reason I got it was to bring me into your orbit so you would marry me?"

"What? No?" he's blustering now. A sure sign that's *exactly* what he thought, and he's embarrassed to be called on it. "That's not what I mean at all. Max's wife is a fucking brilliant lawyer. She was defending Haven Financial against a massive HR lawsuit when Uncle Bill set them up."

Seriously? That's all he's got? Pathetic.

"I don't know Max and his wife, and I don't give a shit about them. As far as I'm concerned, they can join you in hell."

"Layla." Ryan reaches out for me as I turn and storm out of the room, but I don't want to hear it.

I have no idea if he will come out after me. I'm numb as I jab the elevator button, step inside the second it arrives, and travel to the lobby. My name is down for sessions all afternoon, but I collect my coat and purse, walk out of the hotel, and step into the first taxi that pulls up. I text Karly asking to be on the next flight back to LA and ignore my phone as it starts to ring. Ryan, Karly... I don't care. I shove it into my purse and stare out the window, still feeling numb. I'm sure the tears will come, but right now, it's best if they don't.

Hurrying up to our suite, I turn my back on the bed I shared with Ryan and his clothes hanging neatly in the closet. Grabbing my suitcases, I make sure I leave no trace of myself and pack my bags, taking them to the lobby to return my keycard and get a taxi to the airport. Karly has texted me with my flight details, and I stay numb until I'm seated in first class, sipping a glass of champagne and watching the doors close at the front of the aircraft. Only then do the tears start.

Hold My Heart

Ryan

Layla didn't make any of the afternoon sessions and was a no-show at lunch. It's probably best if she has time to calm down. I fucked everything up earlier, but if we're both calm and I can explain, she'll understand. I wasn't doubting her ability. I wasn't. Uncle Bill would never have put an unqualified person in a position of control of one of his companies. Would he scour every Haven entity to find a *qualified* woman with whom he could set me up? I one hundred percent believe he fucking would. And I think he has. I need to explain that to Layla without emotions and shit.

Arriving at our hotel, I stride through the lobby, going straight to our suite on the top floor. Taking a deep breath, I square my shoulders and walk inside. It's eerily quiet. Maybe Layla is having a nap. Tiptoeing through so I don't disturb her, I peek my head into the room. The bed is neatly made and very empty. Shit. She's not here. Maybe she's gone to the bar.

Sighing, I move through to the closet. I'll change and find her. Apologize some more and *explain*. My feet falter as I step into the walk-in closet, my eyes darting around. It's too empty. All of Layla's colorful, prissy dresses are gone. Like, *gone*.

My heart is thudding in my ears as I slowly move around the room, opening drawers and confirming without a shadow of a fucking doubt that not a scrap of lace remains. Fuck. I really shit the bed on this one. Grabbing the bedside phone, I call down to the reception desk.

"Reception, how can we be of service," the woman chirps like it isn't a shitty fucking day.

"I need to know the room Ms. Layla Hall moved to today."

There is a pause as long fingernails tap around on a touch screen.

"I'm sorry, Mr. Pierce Westerhaven. We don't have a record of Ms. Layla Hall in our guest list anywhere but the Presidential Suite."

"Well, she's not here, so where is she?"

"One moment, Mr. Pierce Westerhaven."

There's a rustling, and a male voice comes through the line. "Mr. Pierce Westerhaven? My name is Lance Pike. I'm the duty manager at the front desk. Ms. Hall returned her Presidential Suite keycard earlier today. I have it here at the front desk, or I can have an employee bring it up to the suite?"

My mouth is dry as I clear my throat. "Thank you. I do not need a second keycard."

HOLD MY HEART

Or even a first. I need to find where Layla has gone. Dropping the phone into the cradle, I dig mine out of my pocket, calling her number.

"Hi, this is Layla Hall. I'm sorry to miss your call. Please leave a message."

"Layla. It's Ryan. Where are you? They said you had left the hotel. Call me back."

Groaning, I end the call, hitting Uncle Bill's number with gritted teeth.

"Ryan."

Fuck. He still sounds pissed at me. I don't blame him. *I'm* pissed at myself. As much as I hate inviting Uncle Bill into my personal life – give him an inch, and he'll take a mile – I need to find Layla to ensure she's okay and make this right.

"Did Layla reach out about moving hotels?"

The pause is excruciating. It's like I'm fifteen again and standing in front of Uncle Bill's mahogany desk in the study of his Chicago mansion, receiving the dressing down of my life for getting a D on a paper.

"Why would Ms. Hall move hotels?"

Fuck. My teeth grind together. I didn't want to admit this to him. "Because we're sharing a suite at this one."

The silence stretches again. "And they had no other suites vacant?"

"I don't know their availability. I only know that Layla left this hotel."

Uncle Bill has the temerity to sound amused. Asshole. "I would suggest you find some humble pie inside you and get ready to feast. In the meantime, this will *not* affect your concentration for the remainder of this conference. I expect my CEOs to be professional above all else."

"Message received."

Hanging up, I scrub my face and run my fingers through my hair. This is so fucked up. Uncle Bill is pissed at me, and Layla is gone. This week couldn't get any fucking worse. There is one person who will know where Layla is. But I don't have her number. I call Andy instead.

"Mr. Pierce Westerhaven?"

"I need you to speak with Ms. Hall's assistant and get me her location."

Another pause. I'm getting fucking sick of them. Andy's is full of more unsaid. After all, he knows we're sharing a suite. "I'll ask Karly and call you back."

"Immediately."

"Yes, sir."

Tossing the phone on the bed, I strip off my shoes, socks, and tie, loosening my top button as I shrug out of my jacket and stride around the room. She couldn't have gone far. Surely there are vacancies at close hotels.

HOLD MY HEART

My phone buzzes on the bed, and I dive for it. Andy. "Yes?"

"Uh, Mr. Pierce Westerhaven… Karly said she booked Ms. Hall on a flight back from DC this afternoon. She arrives here in LA in the next hour."

"Fuck!"

Ending the call with Andy, I pull up Layla's number again.

"Hi, this is Layla Hall. I'm sorry to miss your call. Please leave a message."

Shit. Of course. She's on a plane. "Layla. When you land, *call me*. I need to explain."

Hanging up, I flop onto the bed, dropping the phone beside my head as I stare at the chandelier above me. She'll call me back. She has to. So I can explain.

Chapter Twenty-Three

Ryan

Striding out of the arrivals hall at LAX, my eyes land on the suited chauffeur holding a sign reading **Mr. Pierce Westerhaven**. I beeline for him, surrendering my bags, and pulling out my phone. My recent call list is depressing. It's just a screen full of Layla's name with the missed call icon. She hasn't answered my calls all week.

"Home, Mr. Pierce Westerhaven?" the driver asks as I settle into the buttery leather seat in the back of the car.

"No. I need to make a stop."

The driver nods as I give Layla's Encino address. It may be desperate, but I need to see her and ensure she's okay. If I can get her to hear me out… everything will be fine. I stare unseeing at LA as it whips past until we finally pull up in front of Layla's condo. Sliding out, I wait until the driver has returned to the car to ring the doorbell. I don't need an audience for my groveling.

I hear footsteps on the other side of the door, and my heart thuds in my chest. I square my shoulders, getting my explanation straight in my head. But the door doesn't open. Fuck. She's seen me through the peephole, and she isn't

HOLD MY HEART

opening it. She's also not walking away. I would have heard the footsteps.

"Layla?" I call through the door, certain she can hear me. "Please. Just let me in, and I can explain."

"I think you've said enough," she calls through the door, her voice shaky. Shit. Is she *crying*? My stomach twists at the thought, bile rising in my throat. Layla doesn't cry. She fights back. She *slaps* me. She doesn't cry. It's not right for her to cry.

"Layla, please."

"Go away, Ryan. Just… go away."

The bile is in my mouth now, my heart loud in my ears as it crashes against my ribs. My feet are like lead as I turn, slowly walking back to the car. I'll talk to her at work on Monday. She needs more time. That's all. As I approach, the driver jumps out to open my door, nodding and pulling away from Layla's condo as he takes me home.

I barely notice the journey, lost in thought, brainstorming all the ways to get Layla to listen so we can get past this.

"Mr. Pierce Westerhaven. We've arrived."

Shit. Home. I get out, allowing the driver to unload my bags and leave them inside the front door as I tip him and trudge upstairs. I head straight to my bathroom, my eyes lingering on Layla's toothbrush sitting next to mine in the holder. We'll get past this. We will.

Dropping the bags in the walk-in closet, Layla's prissy work dresses and matching shoes catch my attention. As soon as I can explain, everything will be as it should be. Layla will be back in my arms and my bed. This is a misunderstanding, and we can work past it. We can work past everything. We're a fucking amazing team.

Turning abruptly, I head upstairs, bypassing the kitchen and straight up to the roof to pour myself a stiff drink. I stare over the city at the view Layla loves so much, the pleasant heat of the whiskey on my tongue. I miss her. I miss Layla. It's a weird feeling. I've never missed anyone before. Not really. The boys have always been a video chat away. Mom and Dad visit four or five times a year, and I return to Chicago just as much. Uncle Bill is always dropping in, and if I need it, San Diego is a hop, skip, and a jump away, and Timmy's spare bedroom is always made up.

But I miss Layla. And not just sexually. Yeah, I haven't gotten laid since Wednesday, but who the fuck cares about that? We had fun together. I miss having her on the other side of the table, eating her blueberry pancakes for breakfast, and making faces at my hot coffee as she drinks her iced monstrosity. I'm taking her to Italy to introduce her to *real* coffee when all this is over.

My phone buzzes, and I read over the R&D department report. More issues with that fucking junior manager. The department head is flagging that the next step in Layla's mitigation plan has been implemented. The plan we sat downstairs and worked through before she gave me a blowjob to remember in her Victorian nanny outfit. *This* is why we can get through this. I need her to bounce ideas off. My work is better when Layla is challenging me. My *life* is better when Layla is here with me. Nothing else is an option.

Layla

Ryan's feet crunch on the gravel as he walks away, tearing another piece of my heart. I know I told him to, and I wasn't going to let him inside… but it hurts more than I thought it would to hear him walk away. When did things get so complicated? Probably when I went and fell in love with him. How freaking *stupid* could I be? The whole time he thought I only got my job to sleep with him. How fucking humiliating.

I will never forget how my heart crushed in my chest when I heard him interrogate his uncle about that. I know I wasn't supposed to hear, but it's better I know what he really thinks. It hurts like a bitch, but it's right that I know. It is.

Running up the stairs, I crawl back under my coverlet, hugging my knees to my chest as the sobs rip out of me.

"Was that him?"

I jump as Allison's voice fills my cocoon. Shit! I forgot she was on a video call when the doorbell rang.

"Yeah," I sob miserably.

"Oh, babe. What happened?"

"I told him to go away."

"And?"

"And he did!"

Allison sighs as I wail. We both know it was a no-win situation, but that doesn't mean I can't cry about it.

"What are you going to do? You should go to a salon tomorrow and make sure you look amazing for Monday."

"I'm going to work from home," I hiccup. Is it cowardly? Yes. Is it what I need? Absolutely.

Allison sighs again but doesn't contradict me; she just warns, "You'll have to face him eventually."

"Yeah. But not on Monday. I'm not ready."

"Well, when you are finally ready, what will you do?"

I huff a sigh, cuddling a pillow to my chest. "I don't know. I don't know if I can stay here in LA, knowing he doesn't think I got the job for anything else but to have sex with him."

"Who cares what he thinks, babe? He's just one man."

"Just the CEO and a 30% shareholder."

"Okay, so a powerful man. But still, just one man. Plus, 30% isn't a controlling share. You're fine."

"Maybe I don't want it to be just fine."

"Well, what *do* you want it to be?"

"The way it was!" I wail again, burying my face in the pillow.

"It can't ever be the same again. Pick another dream."

Allison's words cut to my core. But she's right. Now I know what he thinks; it can't ever be the same again. I think that hurts worse than anything else.

Chapter Twenty-Four

Ryan

It's been two weeks. Layla hasn't set foot in the office. She hasn't answered my calls, and the two times I've been to her condo, she hasn't even answered the door. I'm going out of my mind. Every day feels like she's drifting further away from me.

I have never minded not being 100% in control of my life before. I studied what Uncle Bill told me to. I went to Duke because he told me to. I moved to LA because he told me to. I like pharmaceuticals. I like LA. I enjoyed Duke. I relinquished control because they were decisions that made my life better. I was always in control of my personal life. Apart from when he ran Sarah off in Kent last Christmas, Uncle Bill has never ventured into my personal life. We had unspoken boundaries, and he always respected them.

The thing is, if he did send Layla here because it was a setup, I don't even care that he overstepped that boundary. Because she was fucking amazing for me. She *is* fucking amazing for me. She makes my life better, both professionally and personally, so I'm okay with relinquishing control. What I'm not okay with is losing her. I'm going out of my mind not being able to contact her. She's cc'd me on a few emails, but it's so impersonal. I've even stooped to sending her an email asking to meet with her, but she didn't respond.

"Mr. Pierce Westerhaven?"

I glance up from where I'm reclining at my desk, my fingers steepled in front of my chin as Andy speaks from the doorway.

"The board meeting is in ten minutes. I'm going there to make the coffee now."

Nodding, I wave dismissively, returning to staring into space. I don't know if Layla will be present. Maybe she'll phone in. At least I'll hear her voice if she does. How pathetic is that? That I'm so desperate to hear her voice, I'll be happy to hear it over the phone. At least I'll know she's okay. Scrubbing my face, I stand, pocketing my phone and making my way to the boardroom. A few members are already there. Lucas is speaking with Georgia Frederickson and Hartley Kemp, and Greta Hawthorne accepts a coffee from Andy.

The rest trickle in as I wait near my chair, sipping – but not tasting – the excellent coffee Andy always provides at these things. The man is efficient, but I hired him for his coffee skills. He also knows every coffee van and food truck in a ten-mile radius at any point. That alone is worth his annual salary.

Lucas approaches with a smile, clapping me on the shoulder as dark hair floats into the room. My heart thuds, falling into the pit of my stomach when I see it's only Helen Lawlor. Why the hell do I feel like a schoolboy waiting for his crush to arrive at the Winter Formal? The door opens again, but it's only Michael Espinoza, so my heart stutters back to life. Fucking hell. I went and fell in love with the woman. Didn't I?

I have no idea when it happened, but it explains why I've been feeling like shit the last three weeks since Layla walked out of that makeshift office. Well, this officially raises the stakes. Now I need to get her back. It's one thing to let a great lay slip through your fingers. It's entirely another letting the love of your life do it. Letting her get away would be unacceptable, and I can't allow that to happen. I won't. Now she needs to show up.

"Time to start, everyone," Lucas calls, checking his watch as he drifts away from me to the other end of the table. What? But Layla isn't here. We can't start without her. I need to see her.

Hold My Heart

Layla

My breath releases in a shaky whoosh as I smooth down the skirt of my purple-striped ruffle dress. I was nervous about this being the dress I wore – after all, it has... blow job memories attached to it – but I need a reminder of that power when I face him again.

My hair is a perfect updo. I spent this morning at a salon, per Allison's suggestion. I also had them do my makeup. It's silly, but Ryan broke my heart, and I'm still in love with him, and this is going to be the first time I come face to face with him since then, and well.... I want to look my best. Is that too much to ask?

My phone buzzes on my bed, and I turn away from the mirror, collecting it and my purse. No bus for me today. I want to arrive looking as perfect as I do now, so I ordered a town car. The driver smiles, holding the door open as I slide inside, checking the time on my phone. I'll make it with time to spare. Good.

I need to spend about ten minutes in my office running through everything I want to say in my mind. I need to have it all straight so that it doesn't disappear from my head the minute I see him.

Why is love so hard? Aren't you supposed to find your person, and it's a nice, steady walk, hand in hand, to the altar?

Ryan and I have never even held hands. How can I be in love with someone and never held their hand? This is so crazy. He's crazy. He drives *me* crazy.

"Ms. Hall. Haven Pharmaceuticals."

The door opens, and I slide out, making my way through the building, smiling and nodding to the people calling out to me, saying how much better I look. I didn't explain my time working from home. "Personal reasons" was all I said. I guess it went around the company that I was unwell. I supposed it's nice of Ryan not to contradict that. He always was more of a gentleman than I gave him credit for.

My heart clenches at the thought. Damn it! I'm supposed to be thinking calming things, not things that make me fall even more in love with him. I'm all cried out. Plus, I'm *not* ruining my perfect makeup with silly tears. There have been enough of them. My stilettos tap on the marble flooring as I cross to the elevator bank and step inside, swiping my access card to hit the top floor button. I hold my breath for every second of the slow ascent. I need to get from the elevator banks to my office without running into Ryan. I'm not ready to face him yet. I need another ten minutes.

I don't know if I'll ever be ready, but it's going to happen, and I want to control how it does. That means hiding in my office for ten minutes. I don't care if it's cowardly. I've been cowardly a lot in the last three weeks, and that's okay. It was

HOLD MY HEART

what I needed to guard my heart and try to sew it back together. But the stitches are new and pulling with every breath. Seeing him might rip them all open again, but I will survive this. I've survived worse. I've had to.

The elevator dings, and I suck in a breath – for courage. Thankfully the hallway is empty, and I hurry to my office, stepping inside the outer room and closing the door firmly behind me. Karly looks up from her desk, shoving away from it and hurrying over to me.

"How are you feeling? You look fantastic!"

"I've been sleeping with Ryan," I blurt out, wincing at how harsh it sounds. Karly blinks at me, her mouth a perfect "o."

"Oh. That would make anyone look fantastic, I bet."

"We kind of broke up. In DC. That's why I came home early and why I've been working from home."

Karly is nodding, wide-eyed, trying to follow along. "Oh, okay. Oh. *Oh*! Today is the first time you're seeing him since it happened?"

"Yeah."

"Okay. Well, don't worry. You. Look. Fantastic. He's going to be eating his heart out."

This is the pep talk I need. This is why I told her about it.

"That isn't all."

Karly looks at me, nodding earnestly again. "I'm all ears."

Good. Because I need to get this off my chest before I go to that board meeting and face him down.

Chapter Twenty-Five

Ryan

The clock is ticking ridiculously loudly, in time with my thudding heart as everyone takes their seats. Andy moves away from the sideboard where he was making coffee, a single iced coffee sitting there. Layla. He intended for her to be here, so she hasn't sent her apologies. Shit. I hope everything is okay. Maybe I should excuse myself and give her a call? Has anyone heard from her? Andy pauses halfway to his seat, returning to the sideboard and picking up the drink.

"Ms. Hall?"

My lungs fill with air as Layla walks into the room, her chin high, looking fucking amazing in the Victorian nanny outfit she wore at my house. That has to be a good sign, right? I half rise out of my chair, dropping back into it when Layla waves the coffee off. Why isn't she drinking it? Layla treats iced coffee like it's manna from heaven. This is off, and I don't like it. Is she feeling okay? There was a rumor going around that she was working from home because she was unwell. I knew better, but maybe there was some truth to the gossip. Shit. I should have sent her flowers or something.

That's always what the Regency guys were doing in the movies Mom used to make me watch.

"Thanks, Andy, but I won't be here long."

What? I'm not the only person staring after her statement. What does she mean, she won't be here long? The board meeting usually takes an hour and a half. Layla stops at her seat beside Lucas, not sitting but resting her hands on the back. Lucas watches her carefully.

"If you could take a seat, Layla, I'll run through the housekeeping, and you can have the floor."

She nods, her shoulders dropping a fraction of an inch. Nobody else probably noticed, but I do. I'm hyper-aware of every movement she makes, and as she sits, hunching in her seat, I mirror her automatically. Shit. I straighten my back. I need to watch myself. Body language is everything at these things. Uncle Bill made all of us boys take a course on commanding body language in high school. It's never let me down since.

One thing not to do is fidget, so I fight the urge to drum my fingers as Lucas runs through the quorum and those present. He skips over the order of business and turns to Layla.

"You have the floor."

She offers him a tight smile, turning to address the table, but in reality, fixing her eyes on the center and not lifting them. A sense of dread and déjà vu creeps through my stomach and up my throat. I don't like where this is going.

"I would like to offer my resignation to the board. Working here has been a privilege and an honor, but I cannot continue."

Helen Lawlor, seated beside Layla, turns to her, placing a comforting hand on her shoulder.

"If it isn't something that can be worked through, I hope you'll let us know how we can help you with your next chapter."

Layla nods, blinking rapidly. Lucas' eyes are pinned to her face. "Please don't feel you need to answer if it's too personal, but can you share why you feel you can't continue? Perhaps there is something this board can do to mitigate any issues."

Layla shakes her head, her lips pressed together. She still hasn't looked away from the conference phone in the middle of the table.

"I'm sorry, Mr. Keller, but I don't think there is anything this board can assist with. I can't work with people who don't respect me and my ability to do my job."

My stomach churns, and I swallow down the rising bile. Hurling isn't an option right now. My heartbeat is the drumming of an army marching through the streets in my ears.

I need to get it under control. I need to get this situation under control. Layla isn't fucking leaving. I can fix this. I have to.

"Layla, everyone here respects you and your abilities," Lucas assures her. Damn right, they do, and Layla needs to understand that. But Lucas isn't the one she needs to hear it from, and we don't need an audience. Maybe here, I can get her to listen to everything I need to say. Standing up, I draw the attention of the table to myself. My voice is lethally quiet, and at least two people actually flinch at my tone.

"Everyone, get the fuck out."

Several looks are exchanged across the table as no one moves. Helen is the first to, shooting Lucas a look as she stands, leaving the room. One by one, the rest of the board leaves until only Lucas remains.

"Layla?" he asks her, not paying me any attention. Her gaze flickers to him, and she nods jerkily. He sighs, his eyes turning on me as he stands. I return his nod, waiting until he has closed the door behind him. Layla is staring at the table in front of her again, not lifting her head. I'm not about to talk to the crown of her hair, so I stride around the table until I'm beside her.

Bending down, I place two fingers beneath Layla's chin to tip her head back so I can finally see her face. My stomach twists like I've been kicked in the gut as her liquid-filled eyes meet mine. Fucking hell. She's trying not to cry.

HOLD MY HEART

Damn it. Spinning Layla's chair around, I kneel in front of her. She's so tiny that our faces are practically even in height when I'm like this. Swallowing roughly, I keep my fingers under her chin, so our eyes stay locked. I need to *see* her hear this.

"Babe." My voice is strained as I start to speak, and she swallows. "I do respect you. I know how good you are at your job. And you're not just good at your job; you make me better at *my* job. My work hasn't been as good without you to bounce ideas off these last few weeks. You make this company a better place. Hell, you make my *life* better."

Layla blinks, a single tear spilling over, which I quickly wipe away with my thumb, keeping my hand cupping her cheek. She doesn't pull away, which has to be a good sign. She doesn't lean into it either, which would have been a better sign, but I have to take what I can get.

"Layla, all these things, and so many, many more, are why I love you."

Her lips part, her eyes widening as I bare my soul. There. I've said my piece. I just hope it's enough.

Layla

Ryan's bright blue eyes are burning into mine. Oh hell. Did he say he loved me? Seriously? Oh my god. This is…not where I saw this day going. I suck in a breath, but all my words have disappeared from my mind. It's an empty shell with only his declaration of love bouncing around. Ryan waits another moment, but when I don't respond, he gives up and uses his hand cupping my cheek to draw my face to his, our lips meeting.

I sigh again, and Ryan groans, his tongue licking into my mouth as my arms snake around his neck. I cling to him, kissing him back hungrily. I've missed this. I've missed feeling close to him. If only my mind would stop racing, and I could lose myself in this moment. Too soon, Ryan lifts his head, his thumb stroking along my lower lip as he presses his forehead against mine, our eyes burning together again.

"Please, don't resign. Haven Pharmaceuticals needs you."

Well, he did say he respected me, and all those nice things about me making him better at his job and making the company better. I mean, that was why I wanted to leave and slink back to San Diego with my tail between my legs.

"I'll stay."

Ryan swallows, his blazing eyes kicking it up a notch. "And give me another chance. I need you too."

HOLD MY HEART

My heart spasms. Holy shit. I need him too, but I had resigned myself to never having that again. Now there's a chance... I'd be crazy not to take it.

"I'll do that too," I whisper. Ryan groans, relief flashing through his eyes as he crushes his mouth to mine again, kissing me until I'm not entirely sure where we are.

Drawing his head back, Ryan presses our foreheads together again with a sigh.

"I want nothing more than to take you to my office and bury myself balls deep in you... but we should probably invite everyone back in and finish the board meeting. We are professionals, after all."

A giggle escapes me, and Ryan flashes me a smile as he stands, bending forward to fix any lipstick smears around my lips. I lift my hand to rub his lips, and he chuckles, turning toward the door.

"I'll let them back in."

He crosses to the door, opens it, and disappears. I stay in my seat, twisting my fingers around. This is the second time I've had an aborted resignation attempt because of my relationship with Ryan. I hope I don't start getting a reputation for being overly dramatic. But they were both very good reasons to offer my resignation. Ryan returns with the rest of the board, who eye me carefully. Lucas nods to Ryan, who returns the gesture, before he turns to smile at me.

"Are we still talking you out of resigning, or did Ryan manage that on his own?"

My cheeks flame as I clear my throat. "I believe Mr. Pierce Westerhaven and I have found a way to work through any issues I might have regarding my standing here at Haven Pharmaceuticals. I would like to withdraw my resignation."

Helen pats me on the hand as Lucas beams, murmurs of appreciation moving around the table, and Hartley, to Ryan's left, claps him on the shoulder.

"I'm delighted to hear that. I want to reiterate whatever Ryan said to assure you that you have the full confidence of this board," Lucas replies, taking his seat.

"Thank you."

"Right. First order of business."

I let out a breath, clasping my hands in my lap as Lucas continues the board meeting. My eyes meet Ryan's, and he offers a smile. It's benign, but his blazing eyes promise me something else when we walk out of here. I press my legs together, trying to ease the throbbing that has started there. I can't wait.

Chapter Twenty-Six

Ryan

After what feels like an age, Lucas finally says those words I've been desperate to hear, "Thank you all for coming today. We'll see you at the next one."

I have to wait for everyone to give Layla assurances that she is welcome here personally, but finally, it's just us. She offers me a seductive smile.

"Your office or mine?"

It's four PM on a Friday. I have a better idea. "If you can wait, I want you in my bed."

Layla's breath catches, and she nods eagerly. That's what I wanted.

"I'll get my car and meet you at the front in twenty minutes." I press a kiss to her lips and leave her to gather her things so that she can meet me out the front. I duck into my office, nodding to Andy.

"Do you still have those tickets?"

"Of course, sir. You said not to cancel until the last minute."

"Great." I hold my hand out as Andy slaps the envelope into it. Tucking it into my inner jacket pocket, I grab my things and throw Andy a smile.

"Take an early day. I am."

"Thanks." Andy grins at me, moving to pack up his things as I leave. When I reach my SUV, my eyes flicker to the empty parking space a few cars down. Layla's space. It's always empty because she doesn't have a car. She should pick one of mine to use. Layla is waiting for me at the front of the building, clutching her purse to her chest. When I pull up, she climbs in, throwing me a smile.

"Hey."

"Hey, yourself," I grin back, pulling out of the compound. The envelope is burning a hole in my jacket, but I keep silent about it. I want to pick my moment. Layla's hand is lying in her lap as she looks out the window. It might be soppy, but I reach over, plucking it up and holding it over the center console. I've never been a hand-holder but holding Layla's hand feels right. Really right. She's still looking out the window as her fingers tighten on mine, but in the reflection, I catch a glimpse of her smile.

Pulling into the garage, I climb out of the SUV and round the hood, helping Layla out. She is walking to the entryway door when I grab her hand, tangling our fingers together to keep her from leaving.

"What?" she asks, her hand gripping mine back as she looks up wide-eyed.

"Which car would you feel most comfortable driving?"

Layla's mouth drops open, taking in the four vehicles parked here.

"Uh, none of them?"

Smirking, I hang the keys to the SUV on the hook near the doorway and tap them.

"You can use the Range Rover Evoque. It's got the best safety features."

Layla giggles, but when she looks away, I catch the insanely pleased look on her face. She leads me out of the garage and up the stairs, but I don't let go of her hand. I'm not ready to stop touching her yet, and Layla doesn't seem to be in a hurry to break the connection either. I guess she's as eager as I am because she leads me straight to the bedroom. As I walk through the door, she turns, dropping her purse on the floor with a thud, and striking a pose. She looks ridiculously mouthwatering in her Victorian nanny dress.

"Anywhere in particular on the bed?" she asks, batting her lashes and looking up at me from beneath them.

My lips stretch into a shark-like grin. "Oh, babe, it doesn't matter. You're going to come all over it tonight."

Layla giggles as I launch myself at her, picking her up and tipping her onto the bed. She bounces as I land on top of her, caging her in my arms, my lips sliding along her jaw.

"God, I've missed you, babe," I murmur against her skin, sliding my lips down as my fingers unbutton her restrictive top, allowing me access. I lift my head to peek at her bra. She's worn her cotton candy pink lingerie.

"My favorite," I breathe as I tug down a bra cup, my lips closing around her nipple.

"They're my favorite too," Layla sighs, wrapping her legs around my waist and pressing her core against my aching cock.

I'd love to watch her move around in these perfect lacy garments, but I need them gracing my floor more. In light of that need, I only pause for a few more moments to give her hard nipples some love and keep moving until she's completely naked; her clothes, shoes, and lingerie in a pile on my floor. My tongue darts out to wet my lips as I savor the sight I was afraid I would never see again – Layla, naked in my bed, exactly where she belongs. My cock twitches, reminding me of my goal. Right. Stripping off my clothes, I come down on top of her again, my lips closing around her left nipple.

HOLD MY HEART

"I know foreplay is the gentlemanly thing to do, but I need to be balls deep inside you, babe," I groan around the sweet bud.

"Yes," she gasps, arching her back to press more of her breast into my mouth. I don't need to be told twice, hooking her legs around my waist as my cock prods her pleading entrance, sliding smoothly inside. She's more than ready for me.

"Such a good girl," I growl, and Layla's pussy spasms around my cock, drawing a strangled groan from my throat.

"I am. I am a good girl," she moans. Yes, she is. To reward her, my mouth leaves her nipple, moving up to suck on her neck as I brace on my forearms, driving deeply into her. I am never letting her go again. How am I supposed to live without *this*? Layla's moans and bucking hips drive my rhythm faster and harder. Trailing my lips from her exposed neck to her earlobe, I bite down on it as she shatters, clinging to me and screaming my name.

Hearing my name ripping from her lips as her pussy clenches at my cock is too much, and I explode with a groan, settling my weight down on her and pressing her into the mattress.

"I missed you, Ryan," Layla whispers, almost too quiet for me to hear, the words muffled against my neck. But I do hear, nuzzling the side of her head and her ear.

"I missed you too, babe."

"Yeah?" She sounds like she's smiling. I know I am.

"Yeah."

Layla sighs as I roll off her, grumbling a little, but I don't want to squish her until she merges with the mattress. I have more plans for her. Looking sated, gorgeously flushed from her orgasm, and more beautiful than a person should be allowed to look, Layla watches as I reach off the bed to grab my suit jacket.

"Do you want me to wear that when I ride you?" she giggles. Uh, yes. I do now I know it's an option. Chuckling, I tap the inside of her thigh sharply, which draws an unexpected moan, Layla's teeth sinking into her lower lip. My cock – though he is spent – twitches half-heartedly at the sight and sound. Okay. That's definitely something to explore. But not right now. All good things to those who wait.

Reaching into the inside pocket, I draw out the envelope, laying the jacket beside Layla on the bed – for her to wear when she rides me later – and tap the side of the envelope against her stomach.

Layla swats at it as she laughs. "What's that?"

"This?" I hold up the envelope, twirling it between my fingers. Layla rolls her eyes at me – ah, I've even missed that gesture – and I grin, handing it to her. "It's for you."

HOLD MY HEART

Her eyes widen, an excited look crossing her face as she opens it, pulling out the two plane tickets. "Tickets to Chicago? The city?"

"Yeah. My dad's sixtieth birthday party is tomorrow night. I'm flying out in the morning. I was hoping you'd come with me."

Layla blushes, even as her eyebrows turn down in a frown, and she turns the tickets over in her hand.

"These are from before DC."

I shrug, tracing a pattern on her stomach with the tip of my forefinger, my eyes following the movement. "I didn't get around to asking you before we went."

"But you didn't cancel my ticket?"

I shrug, lifting my eyes to meet hers with a small smile. "Andy would have canceled tomorrow if you still weren't speaking to me."

Layla nods, turning her attention to the tickets again, her frown long gone and the corners of her mouth tugging up into an adorably teasing smile.

"You want me to meet your family?"

"Yes," I reply promptly and truthfully. I want her to meet everyone important to me. That's what you do when you meet the woman you love, isn't it? "I want to meet yours too."

She sighs, looking at the tickets again, her teasing smile gone.

"What is it?"

She shrugs, her eyes darting to my face. "You're never going to meet my family. Sorry."

What? But I thought....

"*I* don't see my family. My mom took off when I was little, and my dad... he stuck around to see me graduate and drop me at college. I haven't heard from him since."

My heart twists at the matter-of-fact way she says it, with a little shrug.

"So, you have no one?" That's awful. Layla doesn't deserve that. She deserves to be cherished. I will shower her with everything she deserves for the rest of her life.

"Not exactly. I have Allison. She was my college roommate. When Dad didn't show to pick me up from the dorms and didn't answer my calls, she took me home. The Johnsons kind of adopted me. I mean, I was an adult, but they made sure I knew I was always welcome at their house for Thanksgiving and Christmas."

"Well, I want to meet Allison."

"Oh, you will."

Okay. That's a little cryptic. Should I be scared? Layla wriggles out of my arms – that's not okay – and climbs out of bed, picking up her lingerie. My eyebrows shoot up – that's also not okay.

HOLD MY HEART

"Uh, what are you doing? I believe I promised you multiple orgasms all over this bed."

Layla sighs, a look of longing crossing her face, but she shakes her head, waving the tickets at me. "If we're flying out to Chicago at 9 AM, I need to go home and pack."

Oh, yeah. That makes sense. Groaning, I also slide off the bed, collecting my clothes and tossing them in the hamper, though I leave my jacket on the bed. Layla will still be wearing that to ride me later tonight. She watches with amusement as I dress in jeans and my Duke sweatshirt, collecting my neatly packed bags and adding my suit jacket to them.

"What are you doing?"

Isn't it obvious? My eyebrows raise as I stare at her. "Coming with you to your place. You can pack, and then...." I hold up my suit jacket to her peals of laughter.

"All right. Are we getting a town car?"

"You live in a gated complex. I'll drive."

Layla laughs as I tangle my fingers with hers again, leading her to the elevator. This way, I don't have to drop her hand to get my suitcase and suit bag downstairs.

Layla

Ryan's hand is closed around mine, where it is lying on the center seat in the back of the town car. He held my hand almost the entire flight this morning. It was adorable. I peer out the window, watching the brick buildings as we drive through the cold streets. It's approaching winter here in Chicago, and boy, can you feel it.

This is only my second trip to the city, but my first was during a glorious summer. This... not so much. Ryan's fingers tighten on mine, and I glance over, throwing him a smile. Yeah, I'm getting nervous now. I'm about to meet his *whole* family. This is a sixtieth. They're *all* going to be there. Plus, we're spending the weekend here in Chicago, at his parent's house, and flying home on Tuesday. It's going to be... a lot.

"This is it up ahead," Ryan tells me, his hand still tightly holding mine. I peer through the windshield between the seats. Oh. Wow. The car pulls up in front of a huge two-level, red-brick house with a lower basement level with windows peeking out on either side of the sandstone stoop. If it were smaller, it would have a cute "cottage" vibe. But it's not

HOLD MY HEART

smaller. It's huge and screams money. Weirdly, even more than Ryan's gorgeous glass and marble LA hilltop mansion.

The front door opens as Ryan leads me to the stoop, the driver following with our bags. A couple is standing there, watching us with amused faces. The woman looks like how I want to age. She isn't a fan of Botox, fine wisdom lines spreading from the corners of her eyes, crinkling deeper as she smiles. Her hair is mahogany brown, artfully colored, and she's slender, a gorgeous cream sheath dress draped over her clotheshorse figure. The man standing beside her has the same piercing blue eyes as Ryan, and a similar tousled hairstyle, though his hair is shades of gray. He looks like a cross between a university lecturer and a nineteenth-century duke. Ryan's dad is kind of silver fox hot.

We reach them, and they beam at me as Ryan drops my hand to place his on my lower back, subtly pushing me forward. "Mom, Dad, this is Layla. These are my parents, Gordon Westerhaven and Kelly Pierce Westerhaven."

"It's nice to meet you. You have a lovely home." Okay, I'm inwardly cringing. That was awkward. Luckily they're better at this than I am. Kelly Pierce Westerhaven folds me into a tight hug.

"We're so glad you could come. Ryan wasn't sure you'd make it."

"I'm glad I could come."

Gordon kisses me warmly on the cheek when his wife relinquishes me and waves us inside. The driver moves up the steps after us, setting the bags down. Gordon turns to tip him while Kelly leads us further into their stunning home. They might only look on a leafy street, but they more than make up for the lack of a view with the stunning interior of their home. Despite the cold, dreary Chicago weather outside, the interior is warm and full of light. It's like we've stepped through a portal into another world.

The floors are lovely light pine, and the walls block pastel colors with white trim. Splashes of green are dotted everywhere from plants, and all the doors are stark black. This is interior decorating at its finest. I need the name of their decorator to come and do my place. Especially my back porch. Pinterest can't hold a candle to this.

"We've put you both in Ryan's old bedroom. I hope that's okay?" Kelly calls over her shoulder as she leads us up the winding staircase to the second floor. Oh, she's talking to me. Right.

"O-of course. Thank you."

Kelly leads us to the third door off the landing, opening it and smiling as I peer inside.

"We'll leave you two to get settled in and freshened up. Ryan, the tour can wait until tomorrow. People will be arriving for drinks within the hour."

HOLD MY HEART

"Thanks, Mom." Ryan bends so she can press a kiss to his cheek, and she closes the door firmly behind her as she leaves us in silence. Ryan sets the suitcases he grabbed on the bed, flipping his open and moving clothes to the closet. It's built-in, not walk-in, so I guess rich teenagers don't always get fancy luxuries. Ryan catches my grin but doesn't comment as I hurry to hang my clothes.

"The ensuite bathroom is through there." He jerks his chin at another door in the wall across from the foot of the Queen size bed. Okay, so I guess rich teenagers get some luxuries. I peer out the feature window beside the bed. It looks across at a large tree and another house, a crazy distance away, considering we are in the middle of Chicago. When I look down, I admire the courtyard space. The ground at the back of the house is higher than at the front, mainly paved with a basketball hoop and some almost leafless trees on the small patch of grass.

"No backyard?"

Ryan crosses to the window and glances down with a grin. "There was, but Dad could park three cars and a boat in the backyard. He closed it in and dug down for a garage. This was Mom's compromise."

"I see where you got your love of fancy cars from."

Ryan waggles his eyebrows, grinning at my teasing. "It's a nice love to have."

Laughing, I move through to the ensuite bathroom, sighing over the color scheme. I don't think anything looked this way when Ryan lived full time here. It's more of a fancy guest bedroom and bathroom than a teenage boy's domain, but the gorgeous design downstairs is replicated in shades of brown. I don't have time to savor it all. We have to be downstairs in less than an hour. Instead, I settle for a quick shower, before doing my hair and makeup as Ryan showers. He taps my ass as he passes on his way to put on his suit.

"You look gorgeous."

I blush, ducking my head and putting the finishing touches on my makeup, moving back to the bedroom to dress in my deep red baby doll dress. I asked Ryan if he wanted me to get different clothes, but he picked this out from my closet for tonight, so it must be okay.

"Are you nervous?" Ryan asks, zipping my dress up and pressing a kiss against my bare shoulder near the spaghetti strap.

"A little."

"Don't worry. They'll love you. Uncle Bill already likes you, so you're halfway there."

I make a face, grateful when he slips his hand into mine to lead me downstairs. I may cling to it, but you can't blame me.

"Oh good, grab a drink. They're arriving," Kelly calls from near the front door. White-jacketed waiters are circling with trays of whiskey and champagne. Ryan grabs two flutes from one tray, handing me one and situating us near the window. From here, we can see everyone as they arrive.

"That's Dad's brother Harold and his wife, Sharon. They're the twins' parents."

Oh, this is good. I'm glad I'm getting a who's who before they walk in to get introduced. Ryan keeps up the commentary, only pausing when the new arrivals come over to us to greet us. There are names, hugs, and kisses, and Ryan is obviously quite close to his cousins.

I know they all got married this year, and one is called Max, married to Sam. Still, it's all a blur, and by the time I'm kicking off my stilettos and Ryan's thumbs are firmly massaging the balls of my feet as my head tips back onto the pillows, I couldn't tell you a single thing about anyone I met tonight. Oh well, I'm meeting all the important people at brunch tomorrow. Hopefully, that will be less hectic.

Chapter Twenty-Seven

Layla

Ryan flashes me a smile as he slides out of the town car, reaching down to offer me his hand. It's a lot easier to exit a car gracefully when he's half-lifting me, that's for sure. I look up at the restaurant with trepidation. I met everyone last night, but I don't remember them. This will be a little less chaotic, and I hope they like me. These are Ryan's favorite people in the whole world. It's important I make a good impression.

Ryan's hand slips into mine and squeezes. When I look up, he flashes another reassuring smile. "Relax. You made a good impression last night. They're going to love you."

I'm not so sure about that. Still, I take a deep breath, walking with Ryan inside. It's like a rainforest threw up. It's weirdly nice. Plants are climbing the walls everywhere and hanging gardens. The noise of conversation floating throughout the space is dulled and not overwhelming, despite how busy the brunch seating is.

Ryan doesn't even have to give a name. I guess everyone in Chicago knows what a Westerhaven looks like. We're escorted to a large table in the corner, where four couples are seated, with two prams – one of which is a double – parked near them. Everyone looks familiar as we approach, but I can't identify faces. Ryan leads me over, planting me in front of him with his arms resting around my waist as they all rise. Well, all but two.

"These are my cousins, Timmy and David." He gestures to the two light brown-haired men standing beside their seated wives. "Angie is married to Timmy, and that's their son, William."

Angie is a pale, dark-haired woman with warm brown eyes cradling a baby about four months old. She grins, waving awkwardly.

"And Ani is David's long-suffering wife," Ryan cracks as the younger of the two men flips him off. "And their twins, Andrew and Leah."

Ani is about my height – thank goodness, the rest of the group are ridiculously tall – with big blue eyes and masses of light brown hair. She grins at me, with no hands to wave as the twins snuggle against her. David strokes her hair gently before lifting one of the babies and settling them on his shoulder.

Ryan turns me slightly to the other four people – with no babies and what looks like mimosas in front of their plates. These two men are both dark-haired, one almost black with bright blue eyes, the other mahogany brown with warm brown eyes and a neatly trimmed beard.

"Max and Beau and their wives, Sam and Nic."

Samantha is a supermodel. She has to be. She is tall, slender, and gorgeous, with light gray eyes and stunning brown hair. Nic is a little shorter, with tanned skin, shoulder-length dark brown hair, and mysteriously dark eyes. Both women giggle and wave to me, with Nic pushing a mimosa from the center of the table to an empty space beside her chair. I think we're going to be firm friends.

We all sit, with Ryan across from me, Nic to my right, and Tim to my left. David leans across the table from beside Ryan, his eyes twinkling.

"I was wondering who it would be to knock this one sideways," he claps Ryan on the shoulder, "and I have to say... you make sense."

There is general laughter, but I get the sense it's at Ryan's expense, not mine. Ryan shrugs David's hand off his shoulder, taking the baby and cradling it before driving his elbow into David's stomach.

"Oof," David grunts, flipping his cousin off. It's sweet that Ryan took the baby because he didn't want to hit David while he was holding them. But also... watching Ryan cradle the baby is doing funny things to my insides.

He looks at the baby with such a tender look on his face, cooing, and I think my ovaries just exploded. Ah, probably a good thing. I can't go baby crazy at the moment. That is getting ahead of ourselves just a bit.

Hold My Heart

"So, you're not Ryan's usual type."

I glance at Nic, who taps her mimosa glass against mine, winking as she talks low under her breath. My eyebrows rise.

"What's his usual type?" I kind of don't want to know, but also, in a morbid way, I really do.

Nic makes a face. "Supermodels."

Yeah. I didn't need to know that. I mean, it makes sense. But still. I wrinkle my nose, and Nic nods seriously.

"Yeah. They all did the supermodel thing until they saw the light."

My eyes dart around the table. Uh, okay. I mean, Angie is gorgeous, and I did think Sam was a supermodel, but the way Nic is talking, I don't think she is. Ani is cute too, and Nic is way sexy.

"What made them see the light?"

Nic snorts, rolling her eyes and shaking her head. "According to Beau, he thinks their Uncle Bill is picking women for them and setting them up. I don't know if that's true, but we almost broke up because of it."

I sip my mimosa, my mind racing. That's what Ryan thought too. I wonder if they all think that. I wonder if it's true. I thought it was a paranoia of Ryan's or something, but maybe there is some truth to it.

"How did you and Beau meet?"

Nic grins. "Bill Westerhaven arranged for us to be roommates."

Oh. I can see why Beau might have thought she was picked for him. But moving two people into a house together doesn't guarantee they will hit it off.

"And Max and Sam?"

"Haven Financial was being sued. Bill handpicked Sam as the best litigation lawyer he employed and sent her to New York to work with Max."

Okay, now I'm invested. "David and Ani?"

Nic waggles her eyebrows. "Bill picked Ani to redesign Haven Property's whole look. He moved Ani into David's condo to 'get to know him' so she could design the whole thing around his personality."

I don't even have to ask the question; Nic answers it anyway. "Angie was Bill's PA. She accompanied him to England for a five-week vacation with all the boys. She and Tim had a fling that lasted."

Oookay. I think Beau and Ryan are right. It's either a massive coincidence, or Bill Westerhaven set up all his nephews, and they fell for it, hook, line, and sinker.

"What are you two giggling about?" Ryan asks, his eyes narrowed on me. I shrug, taking a sip of my mimosa.

"Girl stuff."

He makes a face, turning to chat with Sam on his other side, and Tim leans toward me with a smile. "I heard you used to work for me at Haven Freight before you moved to LA."

"That's right." It takes everything I have not to throw in a "sir." Force of habit.

"Well, with all the changes for the better you're making at Haven Pharmaceuticals, just know that I'm kicking myself for not discovering you before you were poached."

Ryan is still talking to Sam, but we can all see the smug smirk on his face. Tim grins in his direction but changes the conversation to Christmas. I don't know what Ryan did for Thanksgiving, but I spent it crying in my tub that I was in love with him, and he thought I was... well, the woman his uncle picked for him. Which I may be. So weird.

Ryan

Lifting Layla's dark hair out of her face, I trail my fingers over her cheek, watching her nose wrinkle cutely in her sleep. She blinks awake, taking a moment to realize she's looking at me, watching her sleep.

"Is it early?" she murmurs, stifling a yawn.

"Not for me, but then I didn't stay up all hours last night drinking wine with my mom and looking at old photo albums."

Layla pouts. "I was *not* going to bed until I saw every single baby Ryan photo in existence."

Jesus. That's... unsexy. She'll never have sex with me again. Some of those photos were embarrassing.

"Are you ready to go home this afternoon?"

Layla makes a face. I know what she means. Taking her sightseeing here in Chicago these last few days has been some of the most fun I've had in this city, which is saying something. She stifles another yawn, frowning up at me.

"What?"

"What did you do for Thanksgiving?"

I grimace. I'd rather not think about it. That's when she wasn't answering my calls. It was excruciating.

"I was at home."

"By yourself?"

"Yeah."

She props herself up on her elbow, looking down at me as I stroke her long hair, falling over her breasts.

"I would have thought you would have done a family thing."

Hold My Heart

Sighing, I shrug, rubbing her silky hair between my thumb and forefinger, watching my hand rather than her face.

"Everyone else did. They were here. I cried off."

"Why?" Layla looks confused. I make a face.

"I didn't want to be around happy families because I wasn't happy."

"Why weren't you happy?"

"Because you weren't talking to me."

Layla's eyes widen, and she leans down, pressing a kiss to my lips. I'm about to deepen it when she lifts her head, grinning down at me.

"I wasn't happy either."

"That doesn't make me feel better," I growl. Why would Layla being unhappy make me feel better? "I was an idiot in DC. Forget everything I said. I should never have even thought it."

Layla shifts, sighing and reaching out to stroke my cheek. "I think your uncle picked us for you too."

My brain stutters. She thinks *what*? I blink up at her, staring with my mouth open. "I don't understand."

Sighing again, Layla taps her forefinger against my cheek as she chews on her tongue. "Nic told me how everyone met. How your uncle sent them all to… disrupt your lives. Just like me. I mean… he couldn't know you would all pick us, but he was putting women in your paths."

Confusion and vindication war within me. "I think you got your job because you were the best person for it."

Layla shrugs, giggling as she flashes a grin at me. "Oh, I think that too. But I don't think he interviewed any men for the role, and one day, I'd love to ask him how many women he spoke to until he picked me."

I'm glad she can joke about it because those weeks I thought I had lost her were the worst of my life. Wrapping my arms around her, I drag Layla down to my chest, brushing a kiss over her cheek.

"I don't care if he picked you for me. If he did, I'm glad. I might never have met you, which would have been a travesty. How am I doing on my second chance?"

Layla giggles, kissing me deeply. "You're doing a good job. B+."

I was hoping for a higher grade, but I've learned that Layla is a hard marker. I pepper her face with kisses until she giggles, trying to twist her head away from me. Rolling us over, my cock nudges against her folds. Layla moans, wrapping her legs around my waist and lifting her hips until the tip of my cock slides into her.

"Are you happy with me?" I breathe against her neck. Layla murmurs something I miss, sighing and lifting her hips again. I take the hint, thrusting fully into her.

Hold My Heart

"Yes," she gasps, wrapping her arms around my neck. "I'm happy with you."

I grin against her neck, starting to thrust. I think my campaign to win Layla over is working. I know exactly what my next step will be when we return to LA, but I have other plans for now.

Chapter Twenty-Eight

Layla

Blinking awake, I slip out of bed, ensuring I don't disturb Ryan. He groans, rolling over and burrowing into the sheets, burying his face in the soft pillows. Grabbing my woolen wrap, I tiptoe out of the bedroom, hurrying upstairs to make iced coffee. My eyes immediately find the view, past the huge Christmas tree that Ryan laughed himself to tears when he helped me decorate it. He was terrible. He always *hires* someone to do it. Given that, I'm sure it's looked better in the past.

We did an okay job, but the decorations are a little... lopsided. Sighing, I also set the coffee machine going – for Ryan. He won't admit iced coffee's superiority and sticks to his swill. Gross.

My eyes linger on the small present pile under the tree. It seems a little ridiculous to have a huge tree for the two of us, but a surprising number of presents arrived for us both from his cousins. I was alarmed, but Ryan assured me he sent gifts for them all and their wives and children and that they were "good ones." I think he had a personal shopper pick them out. If he put my name on them, too, I sure hope he did.

HOLD MY HEART

My phone buzzes, and I swipe to answer the video chat, holding up my iced coffee in a salute.

"Bitch, you better have used that cinnamon coffee syrup I sent you!" Allison shrieks through the chat.

"I did! Did you use the hazelnut one I sent you?"

"I did!"

We toast and sip. Mmm, that's delicious.

"Hole in one, *again*. Damn girl, you know your way around an iced coffee."

"Back atcha," I giggle and wink, turning the camera so she can see the view. "Merry Christmas!"

"Bitch, I fucking hate you! That view is to die for."

"I hope she doesn't die. I'd miss her," Ryan rumbles, pulling his Duke sweatshirt over his head as he summits the stairs, waving at the phone I brandish at him. "Merry Christmas, Allison."

"Merry Christmas, Ryan. I suppose you can come on our Mexico girl's trip in the new year."

He blinks, still not fully awake. Stifling a yawn and crossing to the swill machine, he throws me a grateful look as he pours a disgusting cup.

"I'll pass. You two have fun."

"Okay, I approve," Allison giggles. I roll my eyes at her, blowing kisses.

"We'll debrief in the new year and book the trip."

"I. Am. In!"

When I hit the button to end the call, Ryan wraps his arm around my shoulders, dropping a kiss on my upturned face.

"Merry Christmas, babe."

"Merry Christmas."

"Breakfast first, or presents?"

Uh, is that even a question? I shoot him a look of pure horror. "Presents. Obviously."

Grinning, Ryan steers me over to the tree, setting his coffee down and sinking to the floor to pick up presents. "Let's get through them then."

"That is *not* in the spirit of Christmas."

"Do you want to open your presents?" he asks, holding the gift out of my reach.

"Yes!"

"Then pipe down on my commentary."

I pout but hold my tongue and am rewarded with the first gift to open. Maybe all the cousins employ personal shoppers, or perhaps "amazing gift-givers" was on Bill's list for the cousins' wives. Whatever it is, I amass a pile of totally awesome gifts, mostly based on my dress sense – I *need* to know where Nic bought these shoes – and my love of iced coffee.

Finally, there are only two presents left under the tree – most of Ryan's gifts from his family had a heavy baseball and car theme – and I'm feeling decidedly nervous. Ryan picks up the last two presents, weighing them in his hands. Okay. His gift to me is small. Mine is larger. With a glint in his eye, he places mine back down and opens his. Uh, unfair! Lifting the car out of the box, he chuckles, turning the box over in his hands, his eyes lighting up like a little kid's.

"You got me a Maserati remote control car?"

"I even got the number plate to match yours."

"This is fucking awesome!"

I wait patiently as he opens everything, runs to the kitchen to eagerly get batteries, and runs the car once around the kitchen island.

"I love you," he laughs, his eyes still glued on the car.

"Good. I love you too."

Ryan's laugh cuts out, and his head whips around, his eyes wide and shining. Okay, so I've wanted to say it for a while. He said it to me weeks ago. But I was waiting for the perfect time, and Christmas morning felt perfect. Swallowing, Ryan smiles, picking up my gift and placing it carefully on the roof of his new toy car. He drives it slowly until it bumps my knee.

"Special delivery."

God, he's cute in a playful mood like this. Grinning back, I pick up the small gift, tear off the wrapper, and study the small velvet jewelry box. Ryan watches me, slowly reversing his toy car back to his legs.

I'm feeling nervous again, flipping it open. My breath leaves me in a whoosh. "They're gorgeous, Ryan."

My fingers skate over the black pearl stud earrings. These are incredible.

"They're not the only gift."

My eyebrows shoot up, but there is nothing else under the tree. Ryan nods to the box again.

"Under the setting."

Oh! I carefully lift the earrings out with the setting, and my breath catches again. There's a dainty golden key on a necklace, with diamonds winking from the band.

"The key to your heart?" I guess. God, he can be cheesy. So adorable. But Ryan is grinning, shaking his head.

"The key to my house."

This house doesn't have a key lock. It's all fingerprints and codes and stuff. Ryan programmed me in when we got back from Chicago.

"I already have access to your house."

"Yeah, but this key isn't so you have access. It's so you have a key to your home."

My head snaps back up, my eyes drinking in his earnest face.

Hold My Heart

"You're asking me to move in with you?" I squeak in surprise. Ryan laughs, setting his remote next to the car and scooting across the ground until he is close enough to tug me into his lap.

"I can have movers at your house tomorrow morning."

My heart thuds in my chest as Ryan leans in, pressing his forehead against mine.

"Say yes."

"Yes."

Like I was going to say anything else. Ryan's face lights up like... well, like a kid on Christmas morning, and my heart swells. This was the perfect morning.

Ryan

My phone buzzes, and I open WhatsApp, smirking as I see the messages from both Beau and Max.

"What's so funny?" Layla asks, magnanimously pouring me a cup of coffee from the machine without even wrinkling her nose. I hold up my phone, and she leans forward, peering at it, her eyes widening. Yeah, it's kind of funny.

BEAU: Nic's pregnant!
MAX: I'm going to be a dad!

"Is that a twin thing, announcing on the same day?" she asks. Chuckling, I pull up The Boys WhatsApp group, where David is already on it.

DAVID: Aw, cute! You synchronized your announcements.
MAX: No, we didn't! He stole my announcement!
BEAU: ME? You totally tried to steal our thunder!
TIMMY: I think it's cuter that their wives synced their....
MAX: TIMMY!
BEAU: You keep my wife's cycle out of your mouth, Timmy!
RYAN: Congrats, guys. Did you knock em up on the same day too?

Layla snorts, taking her cinnamon iced coffee up to the roof as I grin, sipping my coffee and joining David and Timmy in ribbing them. The twins do a lot of weirdly unexplained psychic stuff... but announcing their baby news on the same day separately is next-level twin weird.

Still laughing at some of the digs David and Timmy are getting in, I set my phone down, my eye catching the coffee Layla made me. Picking it up, my eyes find the view. With Sam and Nic both expecting, I'm not only the only one not married, but I'm also the only one without a kid – or one on the way. There is no sound on the stairs, so Layla must be ensconced up there with her sugary caffeine hit.

Taking my coffee downstairs, I walk into the bedroom, leaving the mug on the nightstand and moving through into the walk-in closet. Opening my cufflink drawer, I pluck out the small velvet box, flipping it open and grinning. The ring I picked for Layla is perfect for her. The band is platinum, with small diamonds studded down the sides. The main event is three cushion-cut yellow diamonds with small white diamond halos. It's a unique ring and will suit Layla's prissy dress sense to a T.

I tuck the ring back into the drawer, close it, and collect my coffee on my way up to the roof. Sure enough, Layla is curled up on one of the wicker couches, sipping her iced coffee and staring at the view. Dropping beside her, I wrap my arm around her shoulders, pulling her against my chest.

"Enjoying your view?"

"I can't believe this is all mine," she whispers reverentially. I grin into my coffee. Oh, babe, you have no idea how true that statement is about to become.

Chapter Twenty-Nine

Layla

"Argh! Have you seen this?"

Allison comes running over, brandishing some organic honey.

"I'm seeing it now," I laugh, batting it out of my face.

"I'm buying it. This is so cool."

Grinning, I wait until Allison makes her purchase and fall in step as we stroll through the beachfront markets. I've been a few times – I even managed to drag Ryan once – but it wasn't as much fun as this. Allison and I *love* markets. Like, you don't understand our affinity to them. Allison links arms with me as our heads move on swivels, taking all the stalls in.

"I'm so glad you're happy, Layla. You deserve it. You deserve it all!"

"Aw, thanks! I am happy, though. I can't believe how amazing my life is."

Allison sighs, sweeping her locs back and making a face. "You sure lucked out. A billionaire. Fancy."

"You're just in love with your room."

HOLD MY HEART

"I am. I may never leave. Did you guys want a live-in housekeeper? I volunteer never to leave that view. I can dust and drink it in."

Laughing, I roll my eyes. For all her protests, Allison loves her job back in San Diego, and I don't think she'd ever move away from her family. She is happy to leave them every once in a while, which is why she has flown here to stay with us for two days before she and I jet off to Cozumel for a week of relaxing on a beach. I can't wait!

"What are you most looking forward to when we arrive?" I ask, leading her toward a smoothie stand.

"Uh, I'm going to get a cocktail as big as my head with a whole fruit salad sticking out the top with a big umbrella."

Okay, that's a plan I can get behind. I even booked us a beachfront cabana for the week we are there. Having Ryan help with the bookings sure greased the process. Who knew? Accepting her smoothie, Allison checks her phone and sighs.

"As much as I'm living for these markets, we need to make waves. I promised Mom I'd video chat her and show her the view at sunset."

"Boo… but also, of course!"

We make our way back to the Range Rover Evoque, which Ryan was serious about making "my car." Allison straps herself in as I pull out of the parking lot, sucking on her smoothie.

"This is the life, Layla. I'm glad you worked things out with Richie Rich."

Rolling my eyes, I reach over to shove her shoulder, turning up the radio as a bubblegum pop song comes on.

"I'm sorry!" Allison wails, dramatically clapping her hands over her ears. "Turn it off. I'll be good, I promise!"

Flicking the station to some soft rock and turning the volume down, I grin, navigating the now-familiar streets. Allison amuses herself by running us through our schedule when we arrive in Cozumel, which involves a lot of cocktails and bikinis and her getting her flirt on. It's a fun way to pass the drive, and I pull into the garage, grabbing the shopping bag as I slide out of the SUV.

"Ooh, I'll take that. I want to show Mom our goodies!" Allison snatches the bag off me, holding her phone up to call her mom as we make our way upstairs. We'll go to the roof, then Mrs. Johnson will get the best view.

"Don't forget to tell her they're welcome to visit anyti-" I cut off with a choke, my eyes wide as I step out onto the rooftop deck. Ryan is kneeling in a sea of flowers and softly flickering candles. Oh. My. My mouth drops open, and I sneak a peek over my shoulder. Is Mrs. Johnson getting a view of this too?

Allison is grinning, and her phone is pointed directly at me. Oh. I don't think Mrs. Johnson is on the other side of that.

Hold My Heart

I think it might be a video. Of this. Which is happening. Like, right now! Letting out a shaky breath, I turn, walking slowly down the petal-strewn path set in the middle of all the flowers. I think he might have an entire florist shop up here. I hope the roof is structurally sound enough to hold the sheer weight of all the flowers.

Ryan is beaming at me when I reach him, a ring box open in his hand. Oh. That's for me. Wow. Just... wow. He reaches for my hand, squeezing it and smiling.

"You drive me crazy, babe. You challenge me and push me and make me a better man. I can't let that go. I can't let you go. You were the best life choice I've ever been handed, and I'm holding on for dear life. I love you. Marry me?"

There are a lot of words on the tip of my tongue, but only one comes out. The only one that matters. "Yes."

Ryan beams, sliding the stunning – huge – yellow and white diamond ring onto my finger and tugging me down to kiss me thoroughly. Somewhere behind me, I can hear Allison cheering, and I giggle against his lips.

"Did you and Allison plan this?"

"Did I ask your best friend to help me propose? You bet your cute little ass I did."

"Well, you nailed it."

"Perfect, because I'm going to nail you later."

And there's my Ryan. I knew he was going to make an appearance at some stage. My arms snake around his neck as I return his kisses eagerly. Behind him, the sun starts to sink over the city. What a perfect moment.

Ryan

Layla jumps, breaking our kiss as Allison cheers again, popping a bottle of champagne. I reluctantly release my fiancée – damn, that feels good – so she can hug her best friend, and they can sigh over the ring.

When I asked Allison yesterday to help me with my plan, she tried to make me show her the ring, but I refused. I wanted Layla to be the first person to see it. Standing, I take the champagne off Allison to pour the glasses while she seizes Layla's left hand in both hers, holding the ring up to wink in the light.

"It's gorgeous, Richie Rich! You really outdid yourself."

I can't say I'm super fond of Allison's nickname for me, but I can wear it. It's true, and it's growing on me. Plus, I am blond.

HOLD MY HEART

"It's so unique," Layla sighs. I wrap an arm around her shoulders to hand her the champagne flute, seizing the opportunity to press a kiss to her temple.

"You're the most unique person I've ever met, babe. You deserve a unique ring."

"Aw, you guys are super cute!" Allison teases, tapping her champagne flute against ours and picking up Layla's hand again.

"You'll have to be careful with that thing in Cozumel. If you set your hand in the wrong direction, the sun's reflection off that huge thing will burn the skin off your face."

Lovely. What an image. Layla laughs, and I think I'm getting used to Allison's outrageous comments. Seeing her and Layla together makes sense. They're like peanut butter and jelly, it shouldn't work, but it just does. A bit like Layla and me. David's comment back in Chicago floats through my mind. I have no idea who they thought I would eventually marry, probably one of the long list of supermodels I bedded, but I bet none of them conjured up someone like Layla. How could they? I wasn't kidding. She is the most unique person I've ever met. There's no one like her, and she's all mine.

That reminds me, when I call Uncle Bill to tell him I'm engaged, I should have a bottle of whiskey delivered to him. After all, whether he admits to it or not, I wouldn't be standing here without his meddling, and my life would be all the poorer for it.

Chapter Thirty

Ryan

My wedding, almost a year to the day after Timmy's at the same Chicago hotel, has yellow flowers. Timmy's had blue. The yellow matches Layla's ring, so it was a good choice. David claps me on the shoulder as the guests start to take their seats.

"Who would have thought he would have gotten us all here within twelve months."

"I would *not* have bet against him."

Uncle Bill sits at the front, next to my parents – Mom is already trying not to cry – with his PA Cathy beside him. I nod to them both, about to turn away when Bill's hand brushes Cathy's leg. Neither of them acts as if anything happened. That's interesting. If I accidentally brushed an employee's leg when I sat beside them, I'd apologize and shuffle to give them space. I wonder how long *that's* been going on.

Turning away, I look around the ballroom space, with the flowers, ribbons, and arch behind me. I wonder if Uncle Bill got a special deal on hosting all five Westerhaven weddings here in the space of a year. He was certainly quick to insist on the place when I told him we were getting married.

My attention is drawn away from the arch when Allison's parents and older brother walk in. I step away from the altar, smiling and kissing Mrs. Johnson's cheek, shaking the men's hands. They're not exactly Layla's surrogate family, but from everything she has said about them, they were the first family to make her feel truly welcome. They will forever have my gratitude for that.

The last of the guests are trickling in. Max and Beau are mirroring their posture, with their arms protectively around their pregnant wives, and Timmy is running double daddy duty with Ani and Angie as David is standing beside me. The music changes, and my eyes snap to the double doors at the end of the aisle, where my whole world is about to walk in. They swing open, and Allison struts through, looking phenomenal in yellow to match the flowers, the color popping against her dark skin.

Then, as the music changes, the moment I have been waiting for my whole life – even if I never realized it until this exact moment – Layla walks in, and the entire world shrinks to the two of us. She looks stunning. Her dress is simple and perfect. I was expecting prissy. This is... not. But it is still all Layla. The off-the-shoulder ivory gown hugs her slim curves to her waist, flaring out to sweep the ground. Her hair is brushed off her face in huge, old-Hollywood waves, with diamond drop earrings reaching down to her collarbones. She is perfection.

Gripping her yellow flowers, her eyes meet mine as she steps into the room, walking herself down the aisle. I have never been prouder of another human being in my life. This is my Layla, strong, independent, and walking toward me, ready to make my life better. Uncle Bill outdid himself when he placed her in front of me.

Layla

I can't believe I'm married to Ryan. This is the greatest day of my life! I'm in a fairytale princess dress, my left hand feels almost heavy with the two rings on it, and Ryan – looking effortlessly handsome with his navy blue three-piece suit and tousled dirty blond hair – stands beside me, his hand resting on my lower back, right where I like it.

"Today has been incredible," I whisper as he leans down, his lips tickling my bare shoulder.

"That's because you're incredible," he murmurs back, tightening his hold on my waist. "I can't wait to see what you're wearing under this."

I bet he's thinking of white garter belts and lacy corsets. The lace is right, and so is the garter belt. The only thing he will have wrong is the color. There's no way he knows I'm wearing his favorite cotton candy pink. *Our* favorite.

"You're in for a treat," I murmur, wondering if he will pick up on the hint. I don't know if he does, but I have to press my legs together as his breath caresses my neck when he chuckles.

"I bet I am. You're such a good girl."

Luckily, my hitching breath is hidden by the arrival of his cousins. Their wives are seated at one of the tables, but the boys have descended on us to backslap Ryan and kiss me. The ribbing ends abruptly when Bill Westerhaven approaches with a beaming smile. They all settle into an easy camaraderie as Bill shakes Ryan's hand and drops a kiss on my cheek.

"It was a lovely day," he assures me. I'm still not used to being *related* to Mr. Westerhaven, so I blush and stammer. Tim saves me.

"I think we all owe you a debt of gratitude, Uncle Bill, for sending such wonderful women our way."

Oh, wow. I didn't think one would just come out and say it. I wonder how Mr. Westerhaven is going to deny it?

Hold My Heart

Snorting into his whiskey, he takes a sip and slowly lowers the glass, his lips tugging into a smirk.

"I had to do something. None of you would have gotten here on your own."

You could hear a pin drop in the silence before all five men howl with laughter. Ryan claps Mr. Westerhaven on the shoulder.

"I never thought I'd live to see the day you admitted you set us all up."

Mr. Westerhaven winks at me, saluting them all with his whiskey. "Never wait for something to happen on its own when you know you can do it better and faster."

There is more ribbing as he strolls off, and Ryan laughs, ducking his head to press another kiss to my neck.

"Let's go sit down," David suggests, his eyes finding his wife over Tim's shoulder.

"Come on," Ryan drags me over to their circular table, taking a spare seat and drawing me into his lap. My eyes linger on the three babies and the two glowing pregnant women. Ryan and I haven't discussed babies, but I think he will make an excellent father. Maybe that's a conversation for our honeymoon.

Laughing at something Max says, I wrap my arm around Ryan's shoulder, pressing a kiss to his temple as he holds my waist. I might have been the bride picked for Ryan, but walking into that office at Haven Enterprises for a job interview was the start of the best days of my life.

Epilogue

Bill

Leaving the boys to chat, I make my way back to Cathy, my extraordinary PA. She smiles up at me as I drop into the chair beside her. She's cradling Andrew, David's young son, as the baby sleeps peacefully in her arms.

"Mission accomplished," she laughs. I grin across at my five happily married nephews, turning back to smile at her.

"Mission accomplished."

"What will you do now?"

I chuckle. What will I do now? Setting those five up has taken up quite a bit of my time over the last two years. Now I'm at a loose end.

"I suppose we could always take that round-the-world trip we were discussing," I suggest. Cathy smiles warmly at me.

"Wouldn't that involve large chunks of time without contact with any of the businesses?"

"I think they've got everything under control," I reply easily with a shrug. Cathy gasps.

"The great Bill Westerhaven is willing to relinquish control?"

Waggling my eyebrows at her, I tip my head at my nephews, who have moved back to their table, each taking a seat beside their wives. Andrew's twin sister, Leah, slumbers on David's chest, and little William sits on Tim's lap, holding up a spoon for his daddy to see.

"Ah, but you see, now they've each married, they are all the better for it."

"Marriage does have that effect," Cathy drawls. I wink at her, my eyes lingering on her bare left hand. The ring wasn't the right size – I'm useless without Cathy doing those things for me – so it's at the jewelry store, being resized. It's just as well. We didn't want to steal Ryan and Layla's thunder tonight.

"I'm certainly hoping it will for me."

Cathy blushes prettily, her left hand flexing as her thoughts turn the same way as mine. Sighing, I sip my whiskey.

"I think they're ready for me to start stepping back."

Arthur, Harold, and Gordon, my three younger brothers, and their wives, Janet, Sharon, and Kelly, all approach, taking their seats at the table. Cathy surrenders Andrew to Janet, his doting grandmother, and Gordon raises his champagne flute.

"To Bill, for helping our boys find what they were missing."

There's much laughter as six more glasses are raised.

"To Bill," rumbles around the table. I smirk at them, reaching over underneath the table to squeeze Cathy's hand.

"Someone had to point them in the right direction," I say with a laugh. It appears there is a consensus at the table on that fact. Glancing over to my nephew's table, Tim catches my eye and raises his glass, my other nephews following suit. Nodding to them, I lean over, my lips brushing Cathy's ear.

"What say we get out of here?" I murmur. She giggles softly.

"I thought you'd never ask," she whispers back. Setting my glass on the table, I reluctantly drop her hand as I stand. I'll make our engagement announcement tomorrow and hold her hand whenever possible. I think my next achievement might be my greatest. It will certainly be my favorite.

The End.

ABOUT THE AUTHOR

Writing has always been a hobby for me ever since I was little. But it wasn't until I took some time off from work to raise my daughter that I really had a little more time to set aside to properly focus on my passion, and bringing the very real people in my head alive on the page.

I find the best way for me to write is to immerse myself in a story, let my characters take me where they want to go, and hope for the best. When finishing a book, I always like to leave my characters at a point in their lives where I know that they are happy, in love, and hopefully, going to go off and live good lives without me looking over their shoulders. I hope that I have managed that!

When I'm not living in the world of my characters, I live in Brisbane, Australia, with my very understanding husband, our wonderful little girl and chilled out son, and our two energetic cats.

K.S. ELLIS

Join my mailing list to receive a FREE novella.

Go to ksellis.com subscribe.

HOLD MY HEART

Find out more about K.S. Ellis' latest releases at ksellis.com

To stay up to date with my work in progress, sign up for my newsletter, or join me on my website for bonus content and advanced access!

Looking for something else steamy to read? Check out the first novella in my Seattle Sizzles collection, Falling For You.

Chapter 1

THELMA

Kill me now. Sighing, I pour the last of the bottle of expensive Chablis into my largest wine glass. Padding out of my kitchen, my bare feet slide over the hardwood floors as I make my way to my main living area. Sinking into the L-shaped camel couch, I draw my knees to my chest, tucking my feet under a throw blanket, and stare out over the blue water of Elliott Bay.

Mom and Dad were horrified when I bought this condo in downtown Seattle. They thought I should have bought a house in the Queen Anne neighborhood – like Artie and Holly – or a condo in Belltown like Pete and the twins. I like living downtown, so I went ahead and bought it anyway.

They were even more horrified when I collected my Harvard law degree and came back to Seattle – not to join the prestigious family sports law firm of Rampwood & Stein, LLP, like Artie and my cousins did – but to join the Public Defender's Office.

Oh my god. You would not believe the tantrums two grown-ass people could throw. There was wailing. *Wailing*. They went through all the stages of grief, but my *god*, it felt like acceptance took a damn long time to come. Bargaining was a fun stage. Mom tried to convince me to join the family firm by telling me about Artie's salary and bonus package. I snort into my wine.

Like that would entice me. I bought this condo out of my trust fund, and enough is remaining that I can buy nice things off the fund's annual earnings whenever I want.

If I were worried about money, I wouldn't have joined the Public Defender's Office in the first place. God, Mom can be so clueless sometimes.

I love where I work. I love the people I work with. I even like some of my clients. Sometimes they aren't the nicest people, but a lot of the time, they just need to catch a break – like all the ones caught by me, being born into one of Seattle's premier families – and their lives would be so different. My time is well spent if I can help them catch even half a break.

Of course, this is America. The system isn't designed to cut breaks unless you're born with them. This is why I'm clutching a wine glass that holds half a bottle, staring unseeing at a gorgeous view.

Leticia Jackson didn't deserve to lose today. She won't deserve the sentence that will inevitably be handed down. I know I can't win them all, but sometimes – like today – it feels like the whole system is a giant boot trying to crush the souls of the people I represent, and my five-foot-six frame isn't enough to hold it off their necks.

Wrinkling my nose, I snatch up my phone, opening an email to Betty Gifford, the CEO of the Rampwood Family Foundation. I send her Leticia Jackson's information. There's not much the Foundation can do for Leticia. Not where she's going. But they can make sure her kids are looked after.

No one in the family knows that Betty and I are helping the families of my lost cases. No one but my sister-in-law, Holly. It was Holly's idea during a wine-fueled cry session after I lost a bad case. A really bad case.

Selma Kepler had been badly abused by her father since she was a little girl. At seventeen, she had enough. She took a kitchen knife and killed him as he slept, passed out in her bed after raping her.

I convinced the judge that twenty years in prison – rather than life – was appropriate. Selma's twin sister Grace was the first person Betty and I helped. The Foundation gave her a fully paid college scholarship to NYU.

My email sent, I drop my phone, turning my eyes back to Elliott Bay as I stare unseeing at the water, sipping at my wine.

JIMMY

"Let's go, ladies! And up! And down! And up! And down! And sprint!"

Casey's enthusiastic voice booms over the sound system. The DJ spins a track as the class pants and cycles, the psychedelic lights swirling around the space, mixing with the incense in the air. It's sensory overload.

My head starts to throb with the pulsing music, the sickly-sweet scent of the incense, and the flashing lights. I'm out. Casting one last glance at the class, I ignore the eye-fucking one of the botoxed-to-the-eyeballs housewives is attempting to give me and slip out of the room.

Hold My Heart

It's quieter once I'm out of the Spincycle class. Casey is doing well. Her enthusiasm is exactly what the class requires, and it's one of our highest earners. We now have three Spincycle instructors, Casey having started almost a month ago. Her probation is up next week, but I'm really happy with her work and how she fits with the culture here.

Making my way past the individual workout classrooms, I hit the elevator bank, swiping my card to access the staff-only upper floor. The elevators are piping out hip-hop today, so Felix must have control of the playlist. Nodding to the familiar song, I step out of the elevator car and stride along the hallway to my office.

Clean lines dominate the space on this floor. Clean lines dominate the whole gym. I gutted the building when I bought it and remade it in line with my vision.

Everyone laughed when I graduated from UCLA and said I was returning home to Seattle to create a fitness empire. They're not laughing now. No, now they all want memberships and mates rates. I guess the dumb jock did make it all on his own.

It was hard. I spent my twenties up to my eyeballs in debt, grinding every second. But now.... Now I'm standing on top of my empire and the fucking world. And I'm only thirty-one.

Striding into my large office, the Dynamo Fitness logo emblazed on the wall across from my desk catches my eye. It never fails to cause a surge of pride to run through me. I was a good-for-nothing dumb jock. Now I'm the CEO of a multi-million dollar fitness empire.

The moment I knew I made it had nothing to do with zeros on a balance sheet or the condo I could afford to buy in Pioneer Square. No. The moment I knew I had made it was two names on Dynamo's membership list. Arthur Rampwood and Beaumont Anders Westerhaven.

Artie Rampwood is one of the famous Seattle Rampwoods. They may have started with sports law, but they're Seattle royalty now. That's how I knew I'd made it in this city.

Beau Westerhaven is one of the five nephews of the elusive Chicago billionaire Bill Westerhaven. Beau runs Haven Publishing, the international publishing house right here in Seattle. That's how I knew I'd made it in this country.

There are other names. Famous singers and actors. Sports stars. Those kinds of names. But Beau and Artie are the two members that mean the most to me. For what they represent.

A knock at the door has my eyes tearing off the dark navy and white of the Dynamo logo. Looking over at the door, I arch an eyebrow at the sight of Mike Hill, one of my boot camp trainers. He is very much not dressed for the class he is scheduled to run in twenty minutes.

Hold My Heart

"Mike. What's up?" My eyes trail over his jean and sweater-clad form. "Air conditioning on the fritz in your studio?"

He frowns, something flickering in his eyes that has me alert, straightening, and turning to face him properly. Mike's unflappable, but right now, he very much looks *flapped*.

"Something's come up with my old man. I need to get to Tacoma."

"Now?"

"Yeah. Sorry. Shit timing, I know."

"Is it something serious?"

"He's had a stroke. Mom's at the hospital with him now."

"Fuck. What are you still doing here? Get on the road now."

Relief washes over Mike's face. He scratches at his head, running his nails over the skin exposed by his dark cornrows.

"I don't know when I'll be back. I have classes."

"I'll cover them. Get going."

"You sure?"

"Yeah, I'm sure. Get out of here."

"You're the best boss ever. You know that?"

"I have my moments."

I wave Mike off as he hurries away. Turning, I pull up his class schedule, running my eye over the class list. Two names stick out. Artie and Holly Rampwood. Shit. I need to bring my A-game.

Mike's a phenomenal trainer. He's dripping with charm and charisma. I'm better at running a punishing schedule. I have made grown men puke, and I have smiled about it. I don't know if I can run a boot camp class like Mike, but I will have to try. Canceling this one isn't an option.